AN Unlikely MATCH

a Regency novel

SARAH M. EDEN

Covenant Communications, Inc.

To Joe,
who will probably never read this

Acknowledgments

THANK YOU TO ANNETTE, HEATHER, Jeff, LuAnn, Michele, and Rob, who keep me from quitting, push me forward, and help me laugh at the insanity of being a writer.

An enormous thank you to Kirk Shaw, who took a chance on me and my writing and whose professional guidance made me a better writer. I'll miss you as my editor, but I am grateful to call you my friend.

My sincere gratitude also goes out to Sian Bessey, who saved me from myriad self-inflicted embarrassments by guiding me through the various Welsh words and phrases found in this book. Anything I got right, I owe entirely to her expertise. Any and all errors are completely my fault.

Thank you to Thomas Gwynn Jones and Sir John Rhys, who wrote wonderfully thorough and captivating books on Welsh mythology and folklore, without which this tale would have fallen irreparably flat.

Last, but not least, thank you to Samantha Van Walraven, whose guidance and expertise I appreciate immensely. I look forward to working with you in the future.

Prologue

England, 1805

It isn't every day an impoverished young gentleman inherits a sizable fortune and an estate. Nickolas Pritchard, not only impoverished and young but a gentleman as well, felt his luck acutely the day just such a remarkable inheritance fell upon him. A roof over his head, even if that roof had the unfortunate tendency to be in Wales, was more than he could have claimed only days before word of the demise of his extremely wealthy, extremely childless, extremely distant cousin had reached him in the London rooms he would have been able to occupy only a few more days, that being when the next quarter's rent was due.

He'd worn black, as the occasion had warranted. He had even attempted to appear somber as his wildest dreams became reality. The solicitor had informed him in a decidedly Welsh accent that he now possessed a fortune amounting to very nearly £10,000 per annum and a home and estate belonging to the Prichard family for more than four hundred years. Nickolas's branch of the family had altered the spelling of their surname during the previous century, something the solicitor assured Nickolas could be overlooked, if not entirely forgiven.

So Nickolas had signed the documents required of him, maintaining an appropriately grave countenance, and had climbed into his newly acquired traveling carriage, destined for the wilds of Wales.

"One thing more I am instructed to tell you," the solicitor had said before the carriage pulled away. "The late Mr. Prichard wished me to inform you, at the last possible moment, that the house you have inherited, though sound in every other way, is, I fear, quite inarguably haunted."

That pronouncement had entertained Nickolas to no end during his journey to his new home. *Quite inarguably haunted.* He had absolutely no worries on that score. As such things as specters existed only in literature and the minds of the easily deluded, he traveled to Tŷ Mynydd, his new home, without the least expectation of finding the place swarming with ghosts.

In one respect, Nickolas was entirely correct. Tŷ Mynydd was not, in fact, *swarming* with ghosts. The house and grounds had only one. And that one, as history or any of his new neighbors could have told him, was plenty.

Chapter One

Radnorshire, Wales—September 1805

ONLY AFTER MORE THAN A dozen staff members had offered an obviously begrudging "*croeso*" in his general direction did Nickolas begin to suspect he was not, in fact, being gravely insulted. It was, he decided, some form of greeting. When he said "*croeso*" to the housekeeper, she looked so very monumentally shocked, he wondered for a moment if he had misinterpreted the mysterious word. Indeed, Mrs. Baines's silver eyebrows shot so high on her forehead they nearly disappeared beneath her starched cap.

"And to you, Mr. Pritchard," she replied with a lingering aura of all-encompassing surprise. "But when did you learn to say such a thing?"

"I will confess here and now, Mrs. Baines, I haven't the slightest idea what I have just said to you." Nickolas very nearly chuckled at himself. "I have heard that word from every person I have met since my arrival and made the rather broad assumption that it was some form of greeting. Was I wrong to think so?"

Mrs. Baines narrowed her eyes, though she didn't look upset or offended. "In the future, Mr. Pritchard, it'd be best not to make so many guesses. Otherwise you may find yourself offending every person you encounter."

It was a rather informal speech from a woman whose employment was not entirely secure, there being a new master of Tŷ Mynydd. Nickolas, however, found he liked her approach very much. She would tell him what was what without feeling the need to sugarcoat anything.

"Do you plan to tell me what it is I have only just said to you, or shall I continue on in my ignorance?" Nickolas smiled at her. His smile had won him an extra slice of bread or an extra helping of stew at any number of inns as he had traveled from one friend's house to another. He'd subsisted on house parties and dinner invitations for years, not caring that he was often invited simply to even the numbers at dinner. An invitation often meant the difference between going to bed quite satisfied or very hungry.

Those days—he smiled to himself—were now in the past. *He* would be a desirable addition to any hostess's guest list. He had income enough to tempt all but the highest-reaching matchmaking mothers. Perhaps even enough—he very nearly sighed out loud—for Mrs. Castleton. For the young Miss Castleton, she of the ebony hair and dark-brown eyes, had caught Nickolas's attention at the beginning of the Season. He'd thought many times in the six months since he'd first laid eyes on the dark-haired beauty that it was a deuced shame he hadn't two shillings to rub together.

"Welcome." Mrs. Baines's voice broke into his thoughts. "*Croeso* is Welsh. It means 'welcome.'"

"And what does *Tŷ Mynydd* mean?"

"Roughly, it means 'house on the mountain,' though you're saying it wrong."

"Am I?"

"*Muh-nith. Tee Muh-nith.*" Mrs. Baines sounded each syllable slowly, pronouncing it precisely.

He tried to copy. Mrs. Baines's expression could have soured a lemon.

"I was that horrible, was I?"

"Welsh is not for the faint of heart," Mrs. Baines responded.

"Do many around here speak Welsh?"

"Only those worth talking to."

Nickolas laughed quite heartily at that. "So the question is, do I attempt to learn Welsh myself and risk offending all and sundry with my inevitable butchering of the language? Or do I relegate myself to the ranks of those not 'worth talking to'?"

"*Are* you worth talking to?" She studied him as if attempting to discern the answer.

It was an impertinence most would not tolerate in a servant. Nickolas enjoyed it immensely. "I certainly hope I am and that my neighbors will agree and accept me to the neighborhood."

"'Tis not your neighbors' approval you should be concerned with," Mrs. Baines said. "Only *her* approval matters." She spoke almost reverently of this person who seemed to require nothing more than a pronoun to identify her.

"*Her?*" Nickolas pressed, intrigued. Mrs. Baines hadn't struck him as one mysterious by nature. He opened his eyes wide, the way he always did when urging the many gossipers of the *ton* to spill their tales. It worked once more.

"Gwenllian ferch Cadoc ap Richard of Y Castell," Mrs. Baines answered.

Nickolas raised an eyebrow in appreciation, both of that indiscernible name and of Mrs. Baines's ability to say the entire thing without pausing to catch her breath.

"Let us hope the lady has a nickname," Nickolas muttered.

"She is known as Gwen," Mrs. Baines said. "And *her* approval of you, sir, is essential to your future here. If *she* does not approve, your life at Tŷ Mynydd will be an endless misery."

A local dragon, then? He would have to do his utmost to butter the old lady up. During his years of poverty—which would be nearly all of his twenty-five years—he had learned a thing or two about charming his way into the good graces of even the most fearsome of society matrons.

"And when can I expect to make the acquaintance of . . ." He opted not to attempt her name, not being sure he had the required several hours such an undertaking would involve. ". . . of Gwen?"

"You will meet her when she chooses to make herself known." Mrs. Baines nodded with crisp finality. "You have met the staff, sir. If you wish, I can show you to the master's chambers, and you can rest before dinner."

"That would be delightful, Mrs. Baines."

"Very good, Mr. Pritchard."

He was, moments later, deposited in his chambers and left to the ministrations of his newly acquired valet. The man made short work of assisting Nickolas from his fashionably snug jacket and laying out an appropriate selection from Nickolas's still-unfamiliar wardrobe—he had obtained a new set of togs with the first of his inheritance—before leaving his new employer to soak in the luxury of a hot bath.

Nickolas's new home was not at all what he had expected. He'd imagined a structure not unlike those of his friends' homes: extremely English and formal. Tŷ Mynydd sat buried in lush, wild greenery amidst rolling hills. He couldn't quite bring himself to call the surrounding landscape mountains, not after visiting the north country, where mountains were indeed mountains. The house itself was cobbled together, not belonging to any particular style of architecture but borrowing from every one imaginable, and a few not quite imaginable. He'd spied a single tower not far from the home, all that remained of what appeared to have once been a fortified castle.

What would his old friends think of his new home? What would the divine Miss Castleton think? Nickolas smiled to himself. Surely her parents could not object to him now.

The Season had come to its inevitable close several months earlier. September in Town, he knew quite well, was very nearly devoid of society. An invitation for a month-long house party would most likely be welcome amongst his associates, filling quite nicely the time remaining before the Little Season reached its height. And it was about time he returned the favor after having sponged off of his share of society for so long. The Castletons would most likely accept. They were already aware, he was certain, of his own preference for Miss Castleton. They might, now that he had the means of supporting a wife, give more consideration to his suit.

He was dried and dressed long before dinner was due to be served and decided to embark on an unguided tour of his home. One could discover far more interesting things without being confined to the formality of being shown about.

The adjoining chamber to his own, Nickolas ascertained, was for his future wife. He smiled at that. If he had his way, it would not be empty long.

He followed the corridor, which quite haphazardly rose or dropped a step without warning and, he felt certain, did not run precisely straight. There were other bedchambers as well. The family rooms, no doubt. Up a flight of stairs, he discovered, quite by accident, the nursery. Down another oddly located staircase, he found another corridor with more bedchambers, likely meant for guests. One, in particular, drew his attention.

It was decorated almost entirely in white. Lacy white curtains draped the bed tucked into an alcove. The coverlet was white as well, with tiny flowers embroidered along the edge. The windows were curtained in sheerest white. A vase with—what else?—white flowers sat on an end table.

It ought to have been an overwhelming sight, far too white and colorless. Instead, the effect proved breathtakingly beautiful. Nickolas stepped inside. He didn't speak a word and found himself working to not breathe any more loudly than absolutely necessary. The room felt more like a church than a bedchamber, as if one ought to be reverent and respectful within its walls.

He walked to the window, watching the scenery through the translucent curtains. The window rather artistically framed the lone stone tower, which appeared not as far distant as it had seemed when he arrived that afternoon. Something about the landscape at Tŷ Mynydd was appealing in its wildness.

Perhaps it was the heretofore unacknowledged drops of Welsh blood flowing through his veins, but he felt almost as if he had lived at Tŷ Mynydd his entire life instead of only a few hours. It felt like home in a way no other place ever had. He had no memories of the home where he and his parents had lived until their deaths when he was six years old. He had been shipped from one relative to another after that until he began at Eton. He'd always been a stranger wandering through the world without a place where he truly belonged. Looking out over the untamed hills surrounding his inherited house, Nickolas felt like he'd finally found his corner of the earth.

A scream brought Nickolas back to the present. He turned toward the doorway, from whence the scream had come. Something about it wasn't the least bit unnerving, almost like hearing a child squeal during a game of hide-and-go-seek.

Sure enough, the producer of said scream was a chambermaid who couldn't have had more than fifteen years in her cup. He waited. If she was anything like the young, barely-out-of-the-schoolroom misses he had more than once been assigned to sit beside, she would soon begin a high-pitched, fast-paced, frantic explanation of whatever it was that had discomposed her.

Five. Four. Nickolas counted silently, anticipating what was, no doubt, coming. *Three.* He heard the poor girl take a deep, shaky breath, her eyes still opened wide. *Two. One.*

Right on cue, she began her explanation, which came out at precisely the pitch he had anticipated but in Welsh. The only word he recognized was *Gwen.* It proved more than enough to pique his curiosity.

He raised his hand to cut off her ongoing monologue. "I am afraid my Welsh is a tad rusty."

"Rusty?" she repeated, obviously entirely confused.

Nonexistent would probably have been a more accurate adjective. "I would appreciate if you would repeat—no, *summarize*—what you've just told me. Preferably in English."

She looked shocked. How many people would berate him over his lack of fluency in the native tongue of an area in which he'd never set foot before that very day?

"Of course, Mr. Pritchard." The chambermaid curtsied. "I only said you were in *her* room, sir. No one ever comes into *her* room. Except, of course, for when we dust and put out the flowers. *She* doesn't like having anyone in *her* room. We know better than to make *her* angry. *She* can be scary, sir. Leastways, I think *she* is. The late Mr. Prichard did too. Most people do. And right wise of them, I say. *She* can be scary, sir. Especially to people *she* doesn't like."

So much for a summary. He wasn't entirely convinced the translation wasn't a few sentences longer than the original version.

"So *she* doesn't like people in *her* room," he repeated, amused in spite of himself. Who was this she? He had a very strong suspicion it was Gwen, whose full name he still refused to even attempt to repeat. Mrs. Baines had, after all, referred to Gwen as *she* and *her* with that same ominous emphasis. It seemed this local dictatress had been a regular visitor at Tŷ Mynydd.

"No," the maid replied, drawing out the vowel, her eyes and mouth forming perfect, wide *O*'s.

It is a lovely room, he thought.

He took another look at the bedchamber as he made his way to the open door. It was astonishingly lovely, in fact. Nickolas fully intended to host a house party as soon as arrangements could be made. The first invitation, he would send to the Castletons. With their home far off in Norfolk, the family would need accommodations at Tŷ Mynydd. Should the delightful Miss Castleton and her family accept the invitation, this beautiful bedchamber would be perfect for her.

"And *she* is rather frightening, is she?" He didn't look at the maid while he spoke so she wouldn't see his amused smile. He didn't want the poor girl to think he was laughing at her.

"Yes, Mr. Pritchard, sir."

An eerie feeling slipped over him, like a droplet of ice-cold water running down his back, between his shoulder blades. It was an unusual experience for him. He generally looked at the world through, as he'd been told many times, rose-colored spectacles.

"What makes *her* frightening?" He glanced back at the maid, who still hovered just outside the doorway.

She appeared startled, confused by his question. Then, in a voice that indicated she thought he ought to have known as much, said, "*She* is a ghost."

Chapter Two

Gwen hovered in a corner of her room unseen, undetected. She did not care to make herself known to this new Mr. Pritchard. Not yet. Such hesitation was unusual for her. The few times Tŷ Mynydd had passed to someone who had not grown up within its walls, she had made a point of introducing herself, with varying degrees of intimidation, to the new occupants within a few moments of their arrival. This Mr. Pritchard, who made an abominable hash of spelling his surname, unsettled her.

Yet, she was inordinately pleased that he liked her room. She could not read minds, contrary to some of the more colorful legends surrounding her four-centuries-long sojourn on the grounds of her family's estate and, therefore, could not be completely certain that Mr. Pritchard was pleased. But she'd seen the gentle smile that had played on his lips when he'd taken his first glimpse, and she'd been unable to prevent an answering one from appearing on her own face.

She was excruciatingly fond of her bedchamber.

In the days when her father had been master of Y Castell, as Tŷ Mynydd had been called during its years as a fortified castle, her bedchamber had been decorated in the heavy brocades and dismal tapestries considered fashionable in the early fifteenth century. She, however, had found them depressing. They weighed down the room, leaving it dark and disheartening. Her father had left the room in that state of dreariness after her death.

When her father died a few short years after her, her uncle had not permitted anything in her bedchamber to be changed, just as her father hadn't, in continued deference to her memory, or some such rot. If he had truly wished to honor her abysmally short life, he might have consulted her on the proper ways in which to do it. It wasn't as if she hadn't been available for a discussion. But, alas, the dearly departed are seldom asked for input in the matter of their own commemoration.

Her uncle's son, her very maudlin cousin Bedwyn, had inherited his father's estate and had adhered to the same ridiculous notion that leaving her bedchamber in a perpetual state of dreariness would make her feel more appreciated. Gwen had never told the two men how very much she would have preferred a drastic and all-encompassing change. Uncle Dilwyn had been deeply affected by the losses in his family, and Gwen had judged it best to simply let him be. It wasn't as if she didn't have the rest of eternity to work out the matter of her oppressive bedchamber. And Cousin Bedwyn grew teary every time she spoke to him.

It really was something of an embarrassment. Her father had been a warrior, though that had led to its own set of problems. She herself had possessed a legendary degree of calm self-possession in the face of drastic, often dangerous circumstances. But Y Castell, for which she had sacrificed so much, had passed into the hands of a bunch of milksops. It had been rather mortifying, actually.

Thankfully for the family name, which at the time was still excessively Welsh, Bedwyn's son had inherited a bit more fortitude than his father. He had grown up at Y Castell and knew Gwen well. So it had been an easy thing to suggest, rather insistently, that her room needed to be redecorated. It had taken nearly a century and an alternating mixture of threats and buttering up, depending on the current master and mistress of her family home, before her room had become what it was then. The soft white had given the room an open, airy feel. It was the only room she was truly at home in.

Most of the original castle had long since crumbled or been demolished. Bits of it remained, cobbled together with the rest of the house. Only The Tower remained intact. Ghosts, Gwen felt certain, were not supposed to shiver, but the mere thought of The Tower made her do just that. It was the one place in all of Tŷ Mynydd she hated.

Perhaps it was the ever-present irony of her very existence that dictated that her room, her refuge, should afford such an unimpeded view of The Tower, which was a place of immense horrors for her. It stood as a stark reminder of that awful time four hundred years earlier. The air inside The Tower still felt suffocating.

Gwen's thoughts turned to the new Mr. Pritchard. It certainly was an abomination the way his family had altered the name. Prichard was bad enough, being a mangled version of "ap Richard," the original, proud Welsh surname her loved ones had borne. But to add that superfluous *T* was tantamount to desecration.

He would bear watching, Gwen told herself. Very close watching.

* * *

A fortnight at Tŷ Mynydd convinced Nickolas he now resided in the most superstitious neighborhood in all the world. His entire staff spoke of "the ghost" with every indication of conviction. Several of the neighboring gentlemen had called on him since his arrival, and he, in turn, had called on their families. It seemed, if the frequency with which the topic arose was any indication, that his neighbors firmly believed in this apparition as well.

"Have you not seen *her*, then?" Mr. Dafydd Evans, the vicar, asked as he and Nickolas spent a leisurely evening in the Tŷ Mynydd library precisely seventeen days after Nickolas's arrival at his new estate.

Et tu, Dafydd? Nickolas silently paraphrased Julius Caesar. They had struck something of an instant rapport when the young vicar had first called, and they were already on a first-name basis. After much practice and a great deal of amused laughter, Nickolas had finally learned to properly pronounce the poor man's name: *Dav-ith*.

Nickolas knew instinctively that they would be lifelong friends. Already, he'd spent several afternoons at the vicarage, and Dafydd had passed several evenings at Tŷ Mynydd. It was good to have a friend in the neighborhood. Even if that friend apparently had absurd ideas about ghosts.

"I cannot say that I have seen *her*," Nickolas replied with a smile. "I hear very contradictory accounts of *her*. I am not at all certain what to think of the ghost I seem to have inherited."

"You do not believe she is real." Dafydd smiled, a look of near pity on his face.

Dafydd was within a year or two of Nickolas's own age. His smile made him appear even more youthful and even less like the starchy curate he remembered from the eighteen months he'd spent with a cousin of his late mother. That man had spent an hour each and every Sabbath warning the congregation of their inevitable arrival in the depths of perdition. The entire parish, it had seemed, was beyond redemption. Nickolas had spent most of those sermons imagining himself off on some adventure or another. He was one of the few congregants who escaped Sunday services without indigestion.

"I admit, Dafydd," Nickolas answered, his own smile growing to a grin, "I don't believe Tŷ Mynydd is haunted." The vicar raised his eyebrow as if amused by Nickolas's lack of belief. "Perhaps it is simply a matter of inexperience," Nickolas conceded. "As you pointed out, I have not actually seen the infamous *she*."

"My understanding of the house's history makes that hard to believe, Nickolas. Gwen doesn't usually wait so long to make an appearance." Nickolas had learned during the last two weeks that Gwen, the ghost, and *she* were not, in fact, three separate individuals but one. "Perhaps she keeps her distance because you are English."

Dafydd was decidedly *not* English. At times his Welsh inflection was so heavy his words became difficult to discern. His declaration did not, however, sound like a condemnation but merely a guess.

Nickolas chuckled. "Perhaps she has not appeared because she does not exist."

Dafydd smiled back. "I hope I am here when she proves you wrong, my friend. I daresay the look on your face will be priceless."

They each raised their glass to the other in amused acknowledgment of the implied challenge Dafydd had issued. Nickolas had declared the ghost nothing more than the overactive imagination of an underentertained neighborhood. Dafydd had declared that Nickolas would eventually have to eat his words.

"I have issued a handful of invitations to a house party I am hosting in a week's time," Nickolas said. "I hope you will join us for dinner and other entertainments while my guests are in residence."

The young vicar's grin turned into something of a smug smile. "I wouldn't miss it," he answered as if privy to some joke Nickolas had not been told about.

"And what is that tone supposed to indicate?"

"You've planned a party without *her* approval," Dafydd said. "Of the party or of you," he added. "You are either very brave or remarkably unconcerned about your own welfare."

"The ghost will object?" Nickolas laughed.

"I imagine you will be made to retract your disbelieving evaluations before the end of your party. In fact, I guarantee it."

"If you weren't an eminently respectable vicar, I would think you were proposing a wager."

Dafydd's mouth twisted in a look of deepest pondering. "A wager?" He even went so far as to rub his chin. "But what should I force you to forfeit when you are proven wrong?"

"That is an awfully cocky statement for a humble servant of the church."

"If I were as *eminently respectable* as you said, I would no doubt ask for a new roof for the church." Dafydd didn't acknowledge Nickolas's last statement with anything more than a twinkle in his eyes. "But I happen to know your estate is already paying to replace the church roof, so it would rather be a waste of a wager."

"True." Nickolas chuckled. Dafydd was enough like him in humor and personality that at times, Nickolas thought him his long-lost, heretofore unknown brother. Of course, one had to overlook the fact that they looked nothing alike. Dafydd's hair and eyes were dark, while Nickolas's were fair.

"And my *eminent respectability* prevents me from wagering actual money," Dafydd continued.

"Naturally," Nickolas replied with feigned gravity.

"I've got it." Dafydd snapped his fingers. "When I win our little wager, you will be required to wear a lady's ball gown to dinner."

"And I suppose when *I* win our 'little wager,' you shall be required to wear said ball gown whilst delivering your sermon the following Sunday."

Both men burst out laughing. Nickolas could just see the very staid citizens of the parish staring in openmouthed shock at their vicar dressed in the very latest in ladies' fashions.

"I think, for the sake of our neighbors' faith and eternal welfare, we'd best choose another means of settling this wager," Nickolas said.

"Not to mention the appetites of your houseguests," Dafydd replied. "Seeing you in a silk ball gown would put even the hardiest of men off his feed."

"Something else, then."

A look of speculation suddenly entered Dafydd's eyes, even as they shifted to the tall windows of the library. "The Tower," he said.

"The Tower?" Nickolas allowed his gaze to follow Dafydd's out the windows and directly to the only remaining piece of what had once been Y Castell. The single stone tower, some two hundred yards from the house, stood as a stark reminder of what, he'd been told, was a rather violent history.

"As you know, I am entirely convinced that the ghost, Gwen, walks the corridors of Tŷ Mynydd," Dafydd prefaced. Nickolas acknowledged the confession with a look of patronizing understanding that was far too theatrical to be taken as anything other than continued lighthearted banter. Dafydd simply shook his head pityingly. "But there are those who believe The Tower is haunted as well. I propose that if you concede my correctness on this matter, which you will inevitably be forced to do, then you shall be required to spend an entire night in The Tower."

"And if not, you shall do so?" Nickolas countered.

"Precisely."

"Is there a time limit on this wager of ours?" Nickolas asked. "I certainly cannot make good on my claim if we must wait until either I concede or you stick your spoon in the wall. Unless I have you entombed in The Tower."

Dafydd laughed as Nickolas expected him to. "You believe, then, that you will never be forced to acknowledge Gwen's existence."

"Certainly not."

"I declare that you will find yourself unable to further deny her existence *in this very house* before your party reaches its conclusion. That is my wager with one night spent in The Tower as forfeit."

"Done." Nickolas grinned and held his hand out to his friend.

Dafydd shook it enthusiastically. "I look forward to seeing you eat your words, Nickolas."

Chapter Three

As a child, Nickolas had known few constants in life. Not one of his relatives had been willing to keep him longer than a few months. He'd found some stability in returning to Eton at the end of each school holiday. And in Griffith Davis, a student his own age whom he met his first year there, he'd found a friend for life. Thus, when he decided to host a house party as master of his own home, Nickolas hadn't hesitated to invite Griffith.

The rest of the Davis family was every bit as welcome. They had offered him a place to live in London every Season until Griffith's sister, Alys, had her come out. Housing an unmarried man who was of no relation to any of them simply couldn't be done with a marriageable daughter under their roof. No matter that Nickolas and Alys were as romantically indifferent to one another as brother and sister, society's thoughts on the situation could not be ignored. Still, Mrs. Davis invited Nickolas to every event hosted at their home and saw that he received regular invitations to take his dinner with the family. She, he often felt, had single-handedly kept him from starving over the years.

Nickolas personally knew Mrs. Davis's abilities as a hostess. Asking her to serve in that capacity for his house party seemed the natural choice. He had to have a hostess. She would manage the thing with grace and capability.

The Davises arrived but a few hours ahead of the Castletons. As the two families constituted the entire guest list, preparations were minimal.

"Welcome to Tŷ Mynydd," Nickolas greeted the Castletons upon their arrival from Norfolk.

"Mr. Pritchard," Mr. Castleton greeted him gruffly in response. Mr. Castleton was not the most social gentleman of Nickolas's acquaintance. He might very well have been the *least* social gentleman of Nickolas's acquaintance.

The party was extremely small by *ton* standards. And to Mrs. Davis's dismay, the numbers would be uneven with Dafydd joining them for dinner each night.

Nickolas made the appropriate introductions between the Castletons and his hostess. All were "delighted," as they were expected to be, and Nickolas began to breathe more easily.

"What a lovely home you have here, Mr. Pritchard." Mrs. Castleton glanced around with what appeared to be appreciation.

Nickolas smiled broadly. It *was* a lovely home. "Thank you, Mrs. Castleton."

She took her husband's arm as they ascended the front steps and entered the house, with Mrs. Davis walking alongside them. Nickolas was left, much to his delight, with the obligation of offering his arm to the divine Miss Castleton.

"We have never been to Wales," she said, her voice as light and angelic as he remembered. "It is truly beautiful."

"I wholeheartedly agree." Nickolas turned Miss Castleton over to Mrs. Baines to be shown, along with her parents, to their rooms.

The housekeeper shot him a very quick look of disapproval, mingled with worry—the same look she'd given him daily since he'd discussed the room assignments with her. Nickolas insisted Miss Castleton be given the white bedchamber he'd stumbled upon on his first day at Tŷ Mynydd. Mrs. Baines had predicted all sorts of dire consequences, most of them muttered under her breath in Welsh, though the tone was unmistakable.

"That is *her* room, Mr. Pritchard," she'd said once more just that morning. "And *she* doesn't approve of anyone being in *her* room."

"Then *she* will simply have to learn to share," had been Nickolas's response.

Mrs. Baines had been grumbling ever since.

The Castletons began their ascent of the front staircase, and Nickolas watched Miss Castleton with a silent sigh. She truly was lovely. And she seemed to genuinely like Tŷ Mynydd. *Wales*, at any rate.

Mrs. Baines and the family had nearly reached the first-floor landing when a sudden wind blew down the narrow stairs. The ladies' hair disarranged and blew about them, their skirts billowing in the stiff breeze. Mrs. Castleton gripped her husband's arm. Miss Castleton gripped her mother. All three pasted themselves rather hastily against the wall that made one side of the stairwell.

The wind died as suddenly as it had begun. No more than a moment's gust, really. But it had not gone unnoticed. Mrs. Baines, at the front of the group, turned accusing eyes on Nickolas, who was watching from the entryway below. It was an *I told you so* look if he'd ever seen one. Each of the Castletons turned to regard him as well.

"Bit of a draft, it would seem," Mr. Castleton grumbled, obviously unconvinced, and shrugged.

"Yes, precisely." Nickolas managed to sound less confused than he felt. "A draft."

A ridiculously strong draft. And a strange, sudden one. Nickolas would have to have his steward take a look at the . . . *At the what?* he wondered. That stairwell was in the middle of the house, no walls abutting the outdoors. The attics, perhaps? But it seemed strange that a draft would enter the house with so much strength from an attic as tall as any room.

"That was odd," Mrs. Davis said to Nickolas, her forehead creased in obvious confusion as she stood next to him. "I have never in all my life seen such a strong, sudden draft."

"Neither have I." Nickolas's eyes followed Miss Castleton's progress from the stairs to the corridor leading toward her room.

"And Mrs. Baines seemed to think you had something to do with it, Nickolas. I know a look of accusation when I see one."

Nickolas tore his gaze away from the upper floor. Miss Castleton had long since disappeared from view. He smiled at his hostess and offered his arm. "Yes, the entire household, you will soon find, intends to blame any little thing that goes awry during this house party on *me*."

"And why is that, pray tell?"

They slowly walked toward the sitting room, where the others were likely gathered. "I made the grand miscalculation of not informing Tŷ Mynydd's resident specter of my plans to host this gathering. The staff, most especially my indomitable housekeeper, are sure of consequences too dire to contemplate. It seems nothing in this house is done without *her* approval."

"The ghost is female, then?" Mrs. Davis looked appropriately amused. "Perhaps you should flash one of the famous Nickolas Pritchard smiles in her direction," she suggested with a feminine chuckle. "I have not known a female yet, be she eight or eighty, who could resist *that*."

"Then how did I manage to convince you to take pity on me and host this ghost-condemned gathering with nothing more than a letter?"

"I am afraid your words were smiling, my dear Nickolas." She laughed, emphasizing the cheery nature of her lightly lined face. "And you flattered my feminine vanity quite unabashedly. How could I resist? It helped, of course, that you were inviting us to your new *Welsh* estate. Mr. Davis could hardly resist welcoming his pseudo-nephew to his own homeland."

Mr. Davis was excessively Welsh, something Nickolas had realized within thirty seconds of meeting his friend's father. The gentleman, who had most likely descended from Welsh warrior stock, swelled with pride whenever his native land was mentioned in conversation and took on a very defensive nature should the comments be unfavorable. Nickolas had managed to look entirely pleased with the location of his windfall when he'd mentioned his good fortune to the Davis family.

"We'll make a Welshman of you yet, Nickolas," Mr. Davis had said, slapping him on the back. The gentleman had nodded his approval repeatedly since arriving earlier that day. He'd spoken to Mrs. Baines in Welsh, bringing the first smile to that woman's face since the house party had been proposed a fortnight earlier.

Mrs. Davis was as English as they came, hailing from Essex. She had, however, come to love Wales nearly as much as her husband, even agreeing to bestow Welsh names on their children, though choosing names that her relatives would be able to pronounce.

"I will admit, Mrs. Davis"—Nickolas lowered his voice conspiratorially—"I was not particularly excited about the location of my new home when I first learned of it. I am finding, however, that Wales is growing on me."

"Ah, yes." Mrs. Davis sighed. "It does that."

The peaceful quiet of the home was quite suddenly rent by a horrified scream.

Chapter Four

NICKOLAS RAN FRANTICALLY UP THE stairs toward the source of the disruption, Mrs. Davis hard on his heels. A second cry followed the first, and though less panic-ridden, it was still worrisome.

He turned down the corridor that led to the guest wing to find all three Castletons gathered outside Miss Castleton's room, the lady in question enfolded in her father's arms and appearing quite disconcerted.

"Calm yourself, Charlotte," Mr. Castleton instructed his daughter. "What has overset you so entirely?"

"There was someone in my room," was the shaky reply.

Mr. Castleton patted her back. "One of the maids—"

"No, Papa. Not a maid. Someone . . . someone else." She motioned toward the open door to the exquisite white bedroom. "By the window. In a white dress. She was . . . f-f-floating!"

"Floating?" Mrs. Castleton looked shocked, perhaps a touch embarrassed.

"Floating?" Mr. Castleton echoed his wife, but with a tone far more intrigued and excited.

"And shimmery." Miss Castleton's voice shook more with each word.

Mr. Castleton turned his eyes toward Nickolas. "Do you have a resident ghost, Mr. Pritchard?"

The man looked positively gleeful. Nickolas barely refrained from staring. "There is a legend about a ghost at Tŷ Mynydd, I understand," he answered diplomatically. But Mr. Castleton did not look satisfied with that explanation. "I am not overly acquainted with the details," Nickolas pressed on. Was the man truly so excited about a ghost story? "Our local vicar, Mr. Evans, will be joining us this evening. He could, I am certain, provide all the details you desire."

"Splendid, splendid." Mr. Castleton put his daughter from him and moved eagerly into the bedchamber she had fled only moments earlier.

The man actually rubbed his hands together in anticipation. So much for paternal concern.

"Are you quite all right, Miss Castleton?" Nickolas asked his delightful houseguest, who still appeared a bit overset.

She nodded, her eyes wide. It would have been a perfect opportunity to offer what comfort and consolation he could, but with her mother standing beside her, such a thing hardly seemed appropriate.

"Would you consider your privacy overly invaded if I were to make a quick inspection of your room—with your parents here, of course—to make certain all is well?"

"I would appreciate that." Miss Castleton nodded, having already attached herself to her mother rather firmly and still looking very nearly undone.

Nickolas wondered fleetingly if Miss Castleton was always so chicken-enhearted. He dismissed the thought as uncharitable, especially when he considered a few tangible benefits of having a ladywife who regularly threw herself into his waiting and comforting arms. He felt certain his smile had grown.

Feeling rather like a hero worthy of an epic poem or two, Nickolas stepped into the room he'd chosen for his damsel in distress.

He made a quick visual sweep of the room but found no one lurking in the corners, other than Mr. Castleton and Miss Castleton's noticeably confused abigail. He certainly encountered not a single person *floating* about or *shimmering*.

Nickolas turned toward the silent abigail. "Did you happen to see what it was that startled your mistress?"

She shook her head. "No, sir. I had only just stepped out on my way below stairs. I came back when I heard her . . . er . . ."

Obviously she worried Nickolas would condemn her mistress's outburst as an excess of sensibility or perhaps a dearth of understanding. He smiled at her, and she blushed, dropping her efforts to explain.

Nickolas tipped his head to one side, eying the window hangings rather closely. They were white, just as Miss Castleton had described the dress worn by her imagined visitor. And when the sunlight hit them just right, the curtains did seem to shimmer. He glanced quickly at the bottoms of the curtains. As he'd expected, they ended several inches from the floor, as if floating above the ground.

He crossed to the window. It was the slightest bit open, no doubt the reason for the occasional rustling of the fabric. Nickolas pulled the window shut, convinced that would put an end to their difficulty.

"I shall ask your vicar about this ghost of yours," Mr. Castleton declared, peeking behind one of the sheer bed curtains. "Int'resting things, ghosts."

Nickolas couldn't recall ever seeing Mr. Castleton so animated. Ironic that his first positive response from the gentleman was on a topic they saw so differently from one another.

"I am certain Mr. Evans will be delighted to discuss her with you."

Dafydd would be thrilled. He would enjoy crowing over the subject if yet another individual was taking his side.

Mr. Castleton rubbed his hands again as he left, obviously reluctantly. Nickolas followed him but stopped at the doorway, glancing back into the room. With the way the shadows played across the window hangings, Nickolas could easily see how Miss Castleton could have thought she'd seen someone there, especially if a light breeze had helped further the belief of movement.

Miss Castleton still stood in the corridor with her hand clasping her mother's arm, watching Nickolas as he emerged.

"Did you find anything, Mr. Pritchard?" she asked, barely above a whisper.

"I believe so. I think the right combination of light and shadows, coupled with a breeze coming through the open window, may have given a very convincing impression of a person floating near the window."

"Then, perhaps there was not a ghost in my room at all?" The hopefulness in her tone was unmistakable.

"That is precisely what I think."

She breathed a sigh of relief and gazed at him with what Nickolas smugly interpreted as something akin to hero worship or admiration. He silently thanked the imaginary ghost and the ease with which its lack of existence was explained.

"Thank you, Mr. Pritchard," Miss Castleton said.

He smiled at her. "It was my pleasure. I will leave you to settle in."

Mrs. Castleton accompanied her daughter inside the room the moment Nickolas left it.

"Well done, Nickolas," Mrs. Davis whispered. "You smoothed over that potential difficulty and managed to offer at least a half dozen of the famous Nickolas Pritchard smiles. No doubt you have made a conquest there."

"Let us hope so."

"The wind blows that way, does it?"

"The wind blows in one direction only, I fear," Nickolas answered. "Mr. and Mrs. Castleton seldom gave me a second glance before my inheritance. I hadn't the means to support a wife, you see."

"As I well know," Mrs. Davis reminded him. "And you are not offended at being accepted now only because of your sudden inheritance?"

Nickolas shrugged, not overly concerned. "I cannot blame her parents for worrying over her future."

Mrs. Davis gave him a searching look, as if she didn't quite believe his declaration.

Nickolas laughed in spite of himself. "If you wish to be offended for me," he said, "then I will not discourage you. But I assure you, I am not in the least upset over their shift of opinion. After all, I doubt they disapproved of me *personally*, only what my circumstances were at the time. And as I disapproved of my poverty as well, I certainly cannot fault them for feeling the same way."

Mrs. Davis laughed too. "What an absurd thing to say."

"One of my talents, as you know well."

They continued companionably toward the sitting room. Nickolas could not imagine being more at ease with his own mother if she had lived beyond his childhood. It was a nice feeling. He hoped his own children would feel the same way with their mother. The thought made him smile all the more.

"I assume you will receive a jaw-me-dead from your housekeeper over this debacle," Mrs. Davis said just before they joined their other guests. "She does seem rather unconcerned over your position as her employer and the risk she takes by offending you."

"She has learned that I am not easily offended. And, yes, she will ring a very smug peal over my head. You see, I was warned not to house any of my guests in that particular bedchamber."

"Were you?" Mrs. Davis looked intrigued.

"It has, apparently, been previously claimed by our ghost," Nickolas explained, feeling a laugh emerging again.

"What a waste of a remarkably beautiful room." Mrs. Davis appeared appropriately outraged and amused. "I am personally pleased you have chosen to place Miss Castleton there. She will be suitably impressed with your home."

Nickolas grinned. "My hope exactly."

"Let us further hope, then, that she does not fancy herself in the presence of a ghost in the future. While her father seemed quite excited at the prospect of a specter, I do not think Miss Castleton shared his enthusiasm."

"I am not worried," Nickolas answered. "As there is not actually a ghost, I doubt we shall have any further problems on that score."

He smiled anew at the thought of Dafydd sleeping in The Tower. That victory Nickolas would happily and loudly crow over. He felt absolutely certain his house party would be an unmitigated success.

* * *

How dare he!

For perhaps the millionth time during her interminable tenure haunting the remains of her childhood home, Gwen rued the fact that she did not have the ability to inflict painful curses on unfeeling people. Else Nickolas Pritchard—whom she had discovered was as *un*-Welsh as possible for someone who was a direct descendant of her own very Welsh grandfather— would have found himself suffering all manner of afflictions for *that* little trick.

No long-suffering haunt should be expected to float through her own bedroom window and find a stranger there. Unpacking. Settling in as if she had every intention of remaining. It was not to be borne!

Gwen had not intended to show herself to the poor creature. She'd come into the room fully visible only because she hadn't been expecting company.

"A pox on Nickolas Pritchard!" she declared with all the fury she could muster.

Had he not acted badly enough, inviting so many strangers to her home—without so much as a word to her, mind you! She quickly cast aside the realization that they had not as yet met, and therefore, securing her blessing would indeed have been difficult. Someone blasted well should have said something to her. She was well known to nearly everyone else in and around Tŷ Mynydd. But no one had bothered.

Then to discover how very English they were, with the pleasant exception of the Davis family, of course. Such a circumstance was not to be taken lightly. Had the English not cost her enough already? Must she now make room for them here? It was all she could do to keep from rattling the walls with her frustration.

Englishmen were positively dripping from the eaves throughout the rest of the house. But she would not have one in her room. Granted, the young lady seemed amiable enough, even if Mr. Pritchard was intent on making a complete and utter cake of himself over her. Oh yes, Gwen had seen him flash that smile of his at her, had seen how his eyes became half hooded when he looked in Miss Castleton's direction. It was pathetic, really.

Gwen sped through the walls until she reached Mr. Pritchard's suite. She would talk to him herself, demand that he remove the interloper from her bedchamber. If she kicked up enough of a gale, rattled the windows, shook the furniture, that sort of thing, he would likely acquiesce. The recently departed Mr. Prichard had sniveled and whimpered in corners whenever she'd attempted to speak sensibly with him. So she'd been forced to use a more take-charge approach, simply making decisions for him and then insisting he follow through with them.

Theirs had not been a comfortable coexistence.

The Prichards were a predictable lot when looked at with a perspective of just over four centuries. On the extreme ends of the spectrum, they produced men who were either hard warrior types or crying babies. There had been one Mr. Cafael Prichard in the eighteenth century whom she'd actually had to knock upside the head with a piece of the family armor, he being one of those ridiculously combatant Prichards. It was a very fortunate circumstance, indeed, that she could kick up quite a wind when need be, as that was her sole means of moving anything.

Where would Mr. Nickolas Pritchard fit on the scale? His line had broken off of the main family line during Cafael Prichard's time, Nickolas's forebear being Cafael's younger brother, Padrig. He'd married an English lass, much to everyone's consternation, and hied himself across the border, where he and his had remained until just a few weeks ago. Gwen remembered Padrig well. He had been far more amiable than his brother, more inclined to smile and laugh, which had annoyed his brother and father to no end. She had missed Padrig but had acknowledged he was probably far happier where he was.

The current Mr. Pritchard had all the family traits mingled in his blood in some combination or another. Gwen had not yet decided where to classify Tŷ Mynydd's new owner—except to classify him as insensitive, unfeeling, and horrid! Giving her room to a stranger. And an English stranger, at that!

She was fairly fuming again. Gwen rushed through the closed door of the master's bedchamber, ready to do battle. She stopped in an instant. Mr. Pritchard was in a semishocking state of dishabille. He was in the process of pulling on a crisp, white shirt but had, thankfully, already donned everything else necessary for the most basic degree of modesty.

Gwen muttered a very unladylike word, forgetting in her shock to keep her utterance silent.

Shirt fluttering into place, Mr. Pritchard glanced around the room, brow creased in confusion. Gwen had never been happier to be invisible. Being caught invading a man's privacy so entirely was not the best way to secure said man's respect and adherence to one's suggestions. Not to mention the fact that if ghosts were capable of it, she'd be blushing horribly.

Bother! No doubt she'd be forced to cosh him upside the head. She so disliked having to be the horribly frightening ghost of Tŷ Mynydd. She had hoped that after enduring the late Mr. Prichard for several decades, the fates would see fit to reward her patience with a master who was far easier to work with at Tŷ Mynydd.

But *this* Mr. Pritchard, with his inordinate fondness for *T*'s and his English friends and his complete lack of respect for the bedchamber she'd worked so hard to make perfect, was a specimen for which she found herself entirely unprepared. He unsettled her in ways no one else had. If her instinct proved right, and it usually did, he was neither combative nor cowardly. But there was something distinctly uncomfortable about being near him.

Mr. Pritchard had turned his attention back to his toilette. His valet reentered the room, hovering nearby with a waistcoat at the ready, while Mr. Pritchard expertly fashioned his neckcloth. Gwen knew she should have left the moment she realized he wasn't entirely turned out for the evening, but he'd regained his modesty so quickly that the need to step out no longer existed.

She moved closer, debating whether or not she should speak to him, whether or not she should make herself visible. She'd never waited so long before. Somehow, it didn't seem like the right moment. The idea, in fact, made her inarguably nervous.

Mr. Pritchard stopped halfway through the creation of his *trone d'amour*, a look of confusion on his face. "Did you hear something, Gramble?" Mr. Pritchard asked his valet.

"Hear something, sir?"

"Like . . . movement."

"No, sir." The valet glanced around the room anxiously, the way new arrivals often did after learning a ghost haunted the house.

Mr. Pritchard made a dismissive noise but still appeared unconvinced. He turned his attention back to his cravat. Gwen slowly slipped back out of the room. She wouldn't approach him yet. But she would have Miss Castleton out of her room by fair means or foul.

That room was all she had left.

Chapter Five

"You are the vicar?" It was as close to a greeting as Mr. Castleton was likely to give.

Dafydd managed to wipe all traces of amusement from his face, though Nickolas knew him well enough to see the twinkle in his eyes. "I am, sir," he replied, even as Nickolas arrived at his side to make the appropriate introductions. The moment names had been exchanged, Mr. Castleton resumed his previous line of conversation with his usual abruptness.

"Tell me what you know of this ghost, Mr. Evans."

Dafydd gave Nickolas a look he interpreted without any difficulty: he was wondering if Nickolas had already admitted defeat in their friendly wager.

"Not a chance," Nickolas whispered.

His good friend, Griffith Davis, stood near enough to hear. He looked between Nickolas and Dafydd a moment. "It seems you've discussed this ghost with the vicar before."

Nickolas smiled. "Yes, and Dafydd wrongly assumes he can make me believe in all that stuff and nonsense."

Griffith had never been the overly talkative sort, but his thoughts showed plainly on his face. His mouth turned in amusement, even as one eyebrow arched with interest. He was obviously looking forward to the battle of wills Nickolas and Dafydd had thrown themselves into.

Nickolas leaned against the mantel to listen to Dafydd's tale. He'd heard very little of the story behind the "ghost" that had caused him so many headaches over the past fortnight.

"There is an entire legend attached to the lady ghost at Tŷ Mynydd." Dafydd spoke with his usual affability. He spared Nickolas a fleeting look of mischief then added, "Perhaps we would be well advised to reserve the telling until the ladies have joined us. After dinner, perhaps?"

"Excellent notion," Mr. Davis said. "A good Welsh tale would be just the thing."

Dafydd nodded. "And it is, I assure you, a *very* Welsh tale. Owain Glyndŵr himself even plays a part."

Mr. Davis's eyes, as well as Griffith's, spread wide at the name of the legendary Welshman. Other than Shakespeare's rather eccentric portrayal of the man, Nickolas knew very little about Glyndŵr. But if he knew Dafydd, which, by now, he felt he did, it would be a diverting tale.

Mr. Castleton looked on the verge of protesting the delay when the arrival of the ladies put paid to his objections. Mrs. Davis and her daughter, Alys, came in first. Mrs. Castleton entered next, her delightful daughter beside her. Nickolas smiled when he saw her, as he always did.

He quickly did his duty as host, introducing Dafydd to the new arrivals. As Mr. Davis had been, Mrs. Davis seemed pleased by the vicar's obvious Welsh-ness, his name and accent making his heritage indisputable. Mrs. Castleton was civil and very nearly friendly but seemed to have dismissed the young vicar almost the moment they'd been made known to one another, precisely the same manner of disregard to which Nickolas himself had been subjected before his inheritance. Despite not feeling offended for himself when he'd been on the receiving end, Nickolas found himself a bit affronted on his friend's behalf.

Miss Castleton, he knew, could be counted on to be charming and not high in the instep as her parents could be at times. He was surprised, therefore, when she allowed Dafydd to bow over her hand but spared him only a passing glance before moving away. She didn't say a word.

Dafydd, Nickolas noted, raised an eyebrow at this pointed dismissal but did not seem offended. If his friend could take this treatment in stride, Nickolas assured himself he could as well. It was, however, a complication he hadn't foreseen. Dafydd would be joining them each evening, the vicarage being a very easy distance from the house. Nickolas sincerely hoped the Castletons would improve in civility.

The group sat to dinner formally, that being Mrs. Davis's preference, which placed Miss Castleton halfway down the table, much to Nickolas's dissatisfaction. It was a small gathering, but she sat far enough away to make conversation between them difficult, if not entirely impossible. Dafydd sat directly to Miss Castleton's right but didn't seem to be faring any better conversationally. She responded to his queries and comments with as few words as seemingly possible. Nickolas felt bad for them both. Obviously each would be more comfortable in the company of someone else. Nickolas fancied himself the *someone else* Miss Castleton would prefer.

Perhaps Alys would make a pleasant companion for Dafydd. Nickolas thought better of it almost immediately. Alys was painfully quiet. He didn't think she'd spoken to him more than a few dozen times in all the years he'd known her. She was more likely to keep to herself.

There was no opportunity for further pondering. Sooner than Nickolas would have expected, the group assembled in the drawing room. The gentlemen had declined to remain behind over port in light of the legend Dafydd had promised the group. Nickolas very nearly laughed out loud. How many anticipated believing the tale, and how many were simply looking forward to an enjoyable interlude?

Griffith sat next to Nickolas and shot him a look of exaggerated solemnity. "The vicar said Owain Glyndŵr is part of this tale. Yours is a very well-connected ghost."

"There is no ghost." He felt certain Griffith knew that perfectly well but still wasn't going to let it drop without needling him as much as possible.

"You also said there was no menagerie at the Tower of London."

Nickolas shook his head at the memory. "That was a very long time ago. And I had never been to London. Surely you can excuse that mistake on the grounds of ignorance."

Griffith shrugged. "Perhaps ignorance is the issue here as well."

"I have a feeling, Griffith, that you and Dafydd will be firmly allied against me in this by the end of the evening."

A sly smile slid over his friend's face. "Perhaps," was all he said.

The small party had all settled in. Dafydd obligingly stood before the fireplace, looking not at all like a vicar. He more closely resembled a mischievous schoolboy preparing to deliver a round tale to his schoolmaster. He looked far too pleased with his position when he glanced briefly at Nickolas. *Drat the man.* Nickolas silently chuckled. Dafydd was gloating at the upper hand he had gained in their wager.

"In the days of Henry IV," Dafydd began almost theatrically, "Owain Glyndŵr, proclaimed Prince of Wales by his countrymen, rose up in rebellion against the English rule of his homeland. Battles were won and lost, castles and fortifications were sieged—sometimes conquered, sometimes forfeited. But one Glyndŵr stronghold was never ceded to the English. The Welsh uprising found invincibility within its walls. In the mighty battle waged for control of the fortress, only one life was lost: Gwenllian ferch Cadoc ap Richard of Y Castell."

"It was a castle, then?" Mr. Davis asked. "*Y Castell* is 'the castle' in Welsh," he added for the benefit of his more ignorant fellow guests and his extremely ignorant host.

Nickolas nodded. He had surmised as much from several conversations he'd had with Mrs. Baines.

"A well-fortified and strategically placed castle," Dafydd confirmed. "Owain Glyndŵr knew this and knew that Henry would realize it as well. Having a devoted ally in Cadoc ap Richard, master of Y Castell, Glyndŵr sent word that Y Castell was under no circumstances to fall to the English. Cadoc vowed he and his people would burn the castle to the ground before handing it over to the enemies of the cause to which he'd sworn his allegiance."

All eyes were glued to Dafydd as he wove his tale. Griffith wore an almost academic expression, as though sorting through the poetic telling, searching for reliable details.

"Anything absurd in the tale thus far?" Nickolas whispered.

Griffith shook his head. "All very plausible."

Plausible, certainly. There are no ghosts yet.

"The castle was reinforced against the inevitable arrival of Henry's forces," Dafydd continued. "Those inside the castle's walls numbered less than fifty. They were dedicated to the battle, determined to defend their home.

"But the King's soldiers arrived, and horror struck the hearts of the defenders of Y Castell, for their opponents stood three hundred strong, armed to a man, well trained, and threatening."

Nickolas held his breath and could see the others in the room do the same. Fifty commoners against three hundred well-trained soldiers. They didn't stand a chance.

"Henry's forces did not attack, did not press the castle. They remained unmoved and waiting outside the castle walls, sure of their victory, awaiting surrender. Two days after their arrival, a black flag was hung from a tower of the castle. In confusion, the English army waited. A white flag would have meant surrender; black was undefined."

A black flag? Nickolas had no idea what that meant. He looked to Griffith for an explanation but received nothing but a shrug in response. Dafydd did not hold them in suspense for long.

"A messenger emerged. The daughter of the house was dead. The occupants requested three days of reprieve before the battle began so that she might be mourned and buried. They were permitted their period of mourning. On the morning of the second day, the sounds of voices raised in song reached the waiting soldiers, who remained confident about their coming victory. But the strains were not those of reverence or mourning; instead, it was a song of battle and victory.

"The siege began and ended in a single day and night of fierce battles. Henry's three hundred were cut down and sent into retreat, numbering, as they fled, less than those remaining inside. Within the walls of Y Castell, the only life lost, the only person mourned, was Gwenllian.

"She became something of a battle cry. An inspiration. Their guardian angel. The king's men returned many times after that but were never able to take Y Castell. And after the Welsh uprising fell and many loyal to Glyndŵr were stripped of their lands by the triumphant king, Y Castell remained in the hands of those who had defended it.

"Legend holds that so long as Gwen stands as guardian of this land, Y Castell—Tŷ Mynydd, as it is now known—stands impervious to invasion, threat of war, or enemy, and will not leave the hands of her family."

"Her family?" Griffith asked.

"The name was anglicized," Dafydd explained. "From ap Richard, the name she and her father carried, to Prichard."

All eyes turned then to Nickolas. "Pritchard?" he repeated. "Then Gwen is my however-many-greats grandmother?" Nickolas could accept that the legendary Gwen had lived, even that she had died during the standoff between royal forces and the Welsh rebels. But he would not concede that she was a ghost haunting the corridors of his home.

Dafydd smiled with amusement. He, no doubt, knew Nickolas wasn't convinced but remained firm in his own conviction. "More like your however-many-times removed cousin. Gwen was her parents' only child and died young and childless."

"How very sad." Miss Castleton's voice broke a little. The tale had obviously moved her. Nickolas unfortunately sat far too distant to offer any comfort beyond a smile of appreciation for her sensibility. "Had she been ill?" Miss Castleton watched Dafydd with gentle intensity, eager for the rest of the tale. It was, Nickolas admitted, an improvement over her earlier coldness.

"The circumstances of her passing are not known." Dafydd addressed his response to Miss Castleton before turning to the rest of the room. "But the house and lands remain in the hands of the Pritchard family."

Nickolas felt the eyes of the entire room glance in his direction. Griffith looked equal parts amused and intrigued. How much of the story he took as fact and how much as legend, Nickolas couldn't say. Indeed, he himself wasn't sure which bits fell under which category.

Dafydd continued. "Gwen resides at Tŷ Mynydd still. It is said that at night she can be seen walking, high above the ground, where the castle walls once stood, standing guard over her home." Dafydd gave Nickolas a look that, if one did not notice the amusement twinkling in his eyes, might have been interpreted as warning. "And she does not take kindly to anyone or anything she perceives as a threat to the home that was defended so fiercely all those centuries ago. She defends Tŷ Mynydd quite singlemindedly and is undeniably loyal to her countrymen."

"Does she object to Englishmen in her home?" Mrs. Davis asked, smiling and obviously unconcerned over her safety.

Dafydd hesitated. It was the first moment of even remote discomfort Nickolas had seen in him. In fact, his demeanor was a little too serious. Nickolas found himself fighting the urge to squirm.

"She does, actually," Dafydd said. "Considering the events surrounding her passing, she has little affection for the English. However"—apparently he noticed that Miss Castleton appeared particularly unhappy with this revelation—"there have been English visitors in the past. I understand one of the former owners of the estate had a son who married an Englishwoman, and the young bride was not mistreated by Gwen."

Miss Castleton gave a smile of relief. Nickolas felt a twinge of jealousy at that smile. She was smiling at Dafydd. She ought to have been smiling at *him*.

"So how do we get this ghost to show herself?" Mr. Castleton asked a little impatiently.

"Never fear, sir." Dafydd's good humor appeared restored in an instant. "There has not yet been a gathering at which Gwen did not make her presence known. She has attended every wedding, every christening, every funeral ever held at Tŷ Mynydd."

"Perhaps I should set an extra plate at dinner from now on," Mrs. Davis said, quite tongue in cheek.

The group laughed at the absurdity of the suggestion.

"Ghosts don't eat," Nickolas thought he heard Mr. Castleton mutter.

Conversation became general after that. Nickolas made his way around the group, as the attentive host he was.

"Mr. Pritchard." Miss Castleton addressed him as he paused in front of her. She even placed a hand on his forearm and lightly pulled him aside. He didn't object.

"Yes, Miss Castleton?"

"Do you think . . . That is . . . Do you suppose I might have seen . . . Gwen?" She actually whispered the name and glanced quickly around the room as if expecting the specter to appear at the mere uttering of her name.

"In my bedchamber earlier? I know you thought it was merely the curtains, but . . . Now I wonder . . . worry that . . ."

Nickolas laid his hand on hers where it still lay on his arm. "Despite Mr. Evans's very diverting tale, I still believe what you saw was a trick of the light. There is no need for alarm."

"But his story was so convincing," she insisted.

"I am certain he intended it to be," Nickolas replied dryly. The more people Dafydd could convince, the more his enjoyment of their wager would increase, no doubt. Nickolas had to admit, however, it was precisely what he would have done were he in Dafydd's shoes. Though Dafydd had done the job better than Nickolas could have hoped to.

"Do you think he intended to frighten us?" Miss Castleton's eyes swung around to Dafydd, where he stood being interrogated by her father.

"No." Nickolas smiled even more. Dafydd wasn't the sort to wish others discomfort—he was simply an enthusiastic storyteller and an underhanded wagerer. "Nor do I think you need to be frightened."

"Thank you, Mr. Pritchard," she said, returning her gaze to his face.

Nickolas flashed one of his famous smiles.

She smiled lightly in reply.

"No more fretting over *ghosts* in your room. There really is no need."

But even as he said it, a strange feeling of foreboding crept over Nickolas. He had a terrible suspicion that his words were overconfident.

Chapter Six

"My apologies," Gwen whispered to the young lady sleeping soundly. "It isn't your fault your host is an unfeeling knave."

Gwen had come to her bedchamber that night as usual, though she had delayed her return for a time, hoping against hope that she would find it once again unoccupied. But there the interloper lay, in Gwen's room, on her bed, even.

It was a shame, really, that Mr. Nickolas Pritchard was making such a mess of things. The young lady, who must have been about twenty—a year in either direction, perhaps—seemed pleasant enough, considering she was English, which was hard enough to overlook, and had a tendency to screech most unbecomingly at a mere brief glance of a ghost hovering at her window. *A little fortitude would do her a world of good*, Gwen thought.

Miss Castleton, for Gwen had managed to learn the intruder's name, slept on, and Gwen set about the business at hand. She kicked up a wind sufficiently strong to open the doors of the room's clothespress, which ought to have stood empty as it had for four hundred years but instead held an extensive wardrobe. Gwen allowed an audible sigh, both of regret at the damage she was about to inflict and of jealousy—she was rather fond of current fashions but had no choice but to don the ethereal gown designated for her the past four centuries.

In a flash, every piece of Miss Castleton's fashionable exterior wardrobe burst free of its confines, swirling in the air before falling, one gown at a time, to the floor below. Gwen had decided quite firmly that humiliating the poor intruder was not necessary and, therefore, left her underthings undisturbed.

Next, she blew out the low burning fire. Late September in this part of Wales could be a bit chilly at night. Each of the room's candles, which were long-since snuffed, she blew behind the heavier pieces of furniture, where they were unlikely to be recovered without effort.

The window curtains were the next target of Gwen's mischief. As she ticked off each item on her mental list, her frustration with Mr. Nickolas Pritchard grew. She severely disliked having to desecrate her own sanctuary in order to reclaim it.

The white sheer curtains, which Gwen was quite fond of and regretted displacing, slipped almost silently to the floor, an upward wind keeping the rod from falling too fast. With a weary shrug, she turned toward the bed. How utterly ridiculous to be forced to such lengths. If Nickolas Pritchard had simply listened to the good advice of his housekeeper, Gwen would not be forced to be such a troublesome apparition.

Again she apologized to the sleeping Miss Castleton, though a smile crossed Gwen's translucent features. She'd developed a talent in her second century of residency in her home and had found it useful many times since. That talent would be just the thing. A gust of wind picked up at the base of one corner of the four poster bed. Up the bed curtain rose, then, as the gust shifted direction, curled back against itself. Up and down, left and right, it twirled, tying in intricate knots.

In only a few moments, all four bed posts bore knotted curtains, hanging lamely and awkwardly. They would be the devil to untie. Gwen hoped the maids would insist that Mr. Pritchard undertake the task. He deserved the struggle it would entail. Somehow, she doubted he would be required to make the effort. Gwen would see to it herself, but she had not yet perfected the art of *un*tying.

She took a quick assessing look around the bedchamber. Just enough chaos to seize the attention necessary without doing lasting damage. Perfect.

Now, to bring her unlooked-for guest to an awareness of the situation.

Rolling her eyes at the absurdity of it all, Gwen floated high enough to hover just above the foot of the bed. The mattress had, of course, been replaced countless times since she had last slept in it. Considering ghosts aren't able to do such mundane things as lie down and relax into a feather bed, it had seemed a rather pointless endeavor by the countless masters and mistresses of the house. Still, Gwen found herself sometimes wondering if it was a comfortable bed. She longed to know for herself, to feel the softness of a down-filled mattress, the warmth of a blanket pulled to one's neck on a chill night. But ghosts didn't *feel* things. Not physically. She still felt emotions: frustration, amusement, loneliness. Mostly loneliness. Hers was a rather lopsided situation.

She couldn't lie down in her own bed, but she could empty her bedchamber. And so what came next was absolutely imperative, even if Gwen disliked the doing of it very much indeed.

*　*　*

It was a shriek worthy of any gothic heroine from the overactive imaginations of the Minerva Press authors. Nickolas was out of bed and on his feet before the echo of it even began to fade. He quickly grabbed a shirt, pulling it haphazardly over his head. He lifted his dressing gown off the chair near the foot of his bed and slipped his arms through the sleeves. As he made his way from his room, Nickolas grabbed a pair of pantaloons, hastily stuffed his legs in them, and followed the sound of a second, equally dramatic cry.

The Davises were standing outside Miss Castleton's door when Nickolas arrived. He could hear some sort of incoherent babbling inside. Nickolas pushed past Griffith, who, despite having proven himself very levelheaded and calm over the years, wore an expression bordering on awestruck.

Good heavens, what had happened now?

He didn't have to wait long to discover the reason for the uproar. Miss Castleton stood on her bed, incomprehensibly swift words falling from her lips as she gestured widely around the room. And the room, Nickolas noted, his own eyes widening, was in such a state of disarray he could not immediately formulate a plausible reason for the chaos.

Gowns lay strewn about, covering nearly every square inch of the floor. Nickolas was obliged to step lightly and deliberately to avoid treading on them. The window curtains were missing, though he could not determine at first glance where amongst the debris they might be. The upheaval changed the very atmosphere of the room. The peace he'd felt the first time he'd stepped inside had disappeared entirely.

"Miss Castleton." He attempted to interrupt the frenzied monologue but to no avail. She continued as quickly and unceasingly as before. Mrs. Castleton, who had come at the scream, appeared to be listening quite intently, though she looked as confused as Nickolas felt. Mr. Castleton was, at that moment, standing with his head buried deep inside the clothespress.

"Miss Castleton," Nickolas tried again.

Her words trailed off as her brown eyes turned to him, wet with tears and wide with apprehension.

Now that Nickolas had her attention, he found himself at a loss to begin. He glanced, dumbfounded, around the room once more. He looked back at his rumpled houseguest and blurted rather gracelessly, "What happened in here?"

"*She* did it." Miss Castleton wrung her hands. "I woke up, and *she* was hovering over my bed. Watching me."

"Good heavens," Nickolas muttered. Now even the divine Miss Castleton was referring to the mythical Gwen by that absurdly accented pronoun.

"The maids told me . . . told me this was *her* room." Miss Castleton visibly paled, swaying a little from her perch atop her bed.

"Do come down, Miss Castleton," Nickolas implored. He could easily picture her toppling to the floor in some semblance of a dead faint.

"Do, dear." Mrs. Castleton added her voice to the argument. "There is something so very vulgar about standing up there."

Vulgar? Mrs. Castleton did say the oddest things at times. She had commented to him some months earlier at a dinner party that one particular young matron's preference for dresses in varying shades of green was "quite unaccountably *low class.*" It often took all of Nickolas's willpower to avoid laughing out loud when Mrs. Castleton was in earnest over some absurd notion or another. Perhaps it would prove beneficial that his estate was in Wales and the Castletons' was across the country in Norfolk. While Miss Castleton was as close to perfection as he could imagine any young lady being, her parents left much to be desired.

As if hoping to prove Nickolas's silent evaluation, Mr. Castleton joined the conversation. "*Her* room, you say?" Mr. Castleton pressed. "The ghost?"

He smiled, seemingly quite pleased with the confirmation.

His wife remained occupied in coaxing their daughter to the ground.

Nickolas refrained from rolling his eyes and tiptoed over the scattered clothing back to the open door. "There seems to be no immediate cause for alarm," he informed the Davises. "I believe you may return to your rooms with no further concerns."

Alys and her parents left, though obviously with reluctance. Griffith remained behind, surveying the scene with furrowed brow and narrowed eyes. A mystery remained unsolved, after all. Griffith could be counted on to help sort it out. Nickolas turned back to what looked like the aftermath of a whirlwind and let out a sigh of confused frustration.

"The bed curtains are knotted," he heard Miss Castleton tell her mother with obvious anguish.

Nickolas's eyes swung to the curtains in question and found them, as she'd described, tied in dozens of knots. The room was, by all accounts, a thorough mess. And Miss Castleton was obviously distressed.

He chided himself for being unsympathetic before. Someone had played her a most underhanded trick. She'd awakened to a state of utter chaos, having no doubt seen the culprit for the briefest of instants during that mind-addling moment before one has completely awoken. Being unduly influenced by Dafydd's tale earlier that evening, Miss Castleton could be excused for being convinced she'd seen something unearthly.

Indeed, the divine Miss Castleton was, even at that moment, dropping dainty tears on her mother's shoulder, having clasped herself to that woman after climbing off her bed. Her distress was moving and guilt-inflicting. She was in his house and had been treated infamously.

"I cannot stay here if this room belongs to a ghost." Miss Castleton sniffed, still leaning against her mother's shoulder. "*She* is angry with me."

"Nonsense, Miss Castleton. Though I hate to even suggest such a thing, I believe you have rather been the victim of someone bent on causing mischief in the name of this fabled ghost."

"That is not any more comforting, Mr. Pritchard," Miss Castleton replied, though she sounded a little less overwrought. "Either way, someone was in my room, doing *this*." She motioned around the chaotic bedchamber.

"I have every intention of discovering who has done this," Nickolas reassured her. "In the meantime, I do not think there is anything to fear. Indeed, I do not truly believe it necessary for you to abandon your room."

A surge of cold air suddenly burst through the room, rustling the knotted bed curtains and swishing the gowns scattered across the floor. Miss Castleton yelped. Her mother gasped. In a flurry of dressing gowns, both fled the room without a backward glance.

Nickolas actually did roll his eyes at that, unable to prevent his impatience from showing. Griffith crossed to the window—the *open* window—and pulled it shut. The wind died the instant he closed it. He gave Nickolas a significant look.

Blast that Dafydd. Surely he knew that his guests would now, like the staff, blame every single unforeseen thing on this ghost he'd so articulately brought to the front of their imaginations.

"I'll stay here," Mr. Castleton declared from behind Nickolas. Turning, Nickolas saw the man look around the room with unmasked excitement. "Do a little research. Keep my eyes open."

"And your daughter?" Nickolas thought Mr. Castleton seemed rather unconcerned that Miss Castleton had just fled the room in a state of near hysteria.

"She's easily startled." Mr. Castleton nodded. "Not so flighty myself."

Nickolas rubbed wearily at his face. A night's uninterrupted sleep would have been nice. He looked over at Griffith, meeting his friend's eye, and motioned him out into the corridor.

"What do you think of our latest otherworldly encounter?" he asked.

Griffith's mouth turned up in amusement. At least *he* hadn't taken Dafydd's tale quite as seriously as the Castletons had.

"Not a ghost?" Nickolas said it as a statement every bit as much as a question.

"More likely someone intent on making you and your guests believe it was." Griffith glanced back at the scene of destruction.

"Dafydd?" Nickolas guessed.

Griffith's brow creased in thought. "Based on my impression of him, likely not."

"One of the servants, then?" He didn't like the idea of his staff playing such a mean trick on one of his guests simply to add weight to a local legend.

Griffith shook his head the smallest bit and made a miniscule shrug.

Nickolas rubbed at the tension in the back of his neck. He was too tired to work through the puzzle. In the morning, the culprit could be rooted out and dealt with. And everyone would finally be brought around to the entirely logical conclusion that Tŷ Mynydd was *not* haunted.

*   *   *

Blast that Nickolas Pritchard! Having Miss Castleton in her room was bad enough. But *Mr. Castleton* was the outside of enough. How could any self-respecting female, even one less than alive, be expected to share her room with a man? Especially one who spent the better part of the night nosing into every corner of the room.

And, Gwen noticed, he didn't make any effort to clean up. Indeed, he quite often stepped all over the expensive gowns spread beneath his feet. The oaf!

Obviously, more drastic measures were called for.

Chapter Seven

NICKOLAS TOOK A TURN ABOUT the grounds with Miss Castleton. He regretted that she'd been so badly treated the night before and offered his most sincere apologies as they walked.

She was as gracious in that moment as she'd ever been during the Season. Though he'd been penniless and perhaps the least sought-after gentleman of her acquaintance, she had never shunned him as so many others had. Her parents were quite certain to ignore his existence, but she was always kind. He liked that she hadn't changed.

"I hope the rest of your stay here in Wales will be more pleasant than your experiences last night," he said.

She smiled sweetly. "I am certain it will, though I am anxious to hear what your vicar has to say on the matter. He seems to be the local expert."

"In that same light, one might say Napoleon is the local expert on the crowning of an emperor."

Her brow furrowed. "You are comparing Mr. Evans to Napoleon?"

He shook his head. "It was a poorly executed attempt at humor, Miss Castleton." They continued along the gravel path winding along the back of the house. "Mr. Evans is by far the most knowledgeable person hereabout in terms of local history and legends."

"We must make certain to ask him what he thinks of last night's events," Miss Castleton said.

For his part, Nickolas knew full well what Dafydd would "think" of all that had happened. Though he felt certain his friend had no part in orchestrating the chaos, he was equally sure Dafydd would not hesitate to present the situation as proof of the ghost he insisted walked the corridors.

"You have a beautiful home, Mr. Pritchard." Miss Castleton looked about her appreciatively.

"Yes, I have grown quite fond of it myself."

The garden path wound back on itself, keeping their leisurely stroll within full view of the drawing room windows. Nickolas glanced up at the windows to see Mrs. Castleton watching them with what appeared to be satisfaction. A few short months earlier, he would not have dreamed such a thing possible. In his poverty, he'd been granted nothing beyond a dance or two over the entire Season. Now he was allowed—encouraged even—to pursue her. How quickly the situation had changed.

They walked on for a quarter of an hour longer, speaking of inconsequential things. Miss Castleton's conversation was enjoyable, her disposition tranquil. More than once she spoke of the beauty around them. Nickolas could not have been more pleased, both that he enjoyed her company as much as he'd expected to and that she seemed to genuinely appreciate his home.

By the time they parted company to change for dinner, Nickolas was entirely satisfied with the progress he'd made. If only he could think of a means of convincing Dafydd to quit filling his guest's mind with ghosts and legends.

* * *

"Nickolas, tell me you did not place one of your guests in the white bedchamber." To Nickolas's confusion, Dafydd actually looked concerned, almost alarmed. "I am certain, *certain*, Mrs. Baines would not have failed to inform you that the white bedchamber is Gwen's."

Mr. Castleton listened raptly, no doubt catching every ridiculous word.

"This nonsense has to stop, Dafydd," Nickolas answered. "You have very nearly frightened Miss Castleton out of her wits."

Dafydd's gaze slipped in the young lady's direction. She listened rather closely but appeared far less excited than her father.

"Last night's mischief upset her quite profoundly," Nickolas said, knowing he ought to make more of an effort to make amends to his houseguest beyond his earlier apologies, though he still found himself occasionally wishing she'd approached the problem with a little more fortitude.

"Forgive me, Miss Castleton, if I unduly alarmed you," Dafydd said, crossing to where she stood. "Gwen can be forceful at times, but I do not wish you to be overset."

"Not exactly what I had in mind," Nickolas muttered. Why would not Dafydd give up this ridiculous game of his?

"I do not wish to upset *her*," Miss Castleton answered, not quite looking at Dafydd.

"She is rather insistent about her room," Dafydd said. "That wing is part of the original castle. And that room was hers during her lifetime. She does not like it to be disturbed."

"I do believe you have taken this too far," Nickolas interrupted. "As a story and a legend, it is diverting, I admit. But you push too much."

"You still do not believe me?" Dafydd raised an eyebrow.

Nickolas gave him a look of exasperation. Of course he did not believe such a taradiddle.

"Tell me this: was anything in the room tied in knots?" Dafydd asked.

"The bed curtains." A slight tremor shook Miss Castleton's voice.

"That is one of Gwen's signature tricks," Dafydd said. "And unaccounted-for gusts of wind."

"Precisely what we felt." Mr. Castleton nodded emphatically.

Nickolas shook his head. He refused to believe anything so ridiculous. Griffith, however, looked intrigued. Surely a gentleman of Griffith's intelligent and logical nature could see how ridiculous the idea was.

"Don't tell me you are beginning to believe this nonsense?"

Griffith didn't look convinced one way or the other. He simply watched them all.

Miss Castleton, to Nickolas's disappointment, was entirely taken in. Did she not question the strange story even a little? Was he the only sane person left in the room?

"Has Mr. Pritchard provided you with an alternate bedchamber, Miss Castleton?" Dafydd asked.

A slight flush spread across the young lady's cheeks. Nickolas very nearly smiled at his friend's faux pas. Sleeping arrangements were not generally discussed in the drawing room over postsupper tea.

"He has, Mr. Evans."

"Then I believe you need not worry over Gwen causing further mischief for you," Dafydd said, explaining the reason for the unconventional turn of his conversation. "Your host, however, may not be entirely in the clear. I believe he has made an enemy." Dafydd shot Nickolas a look of warning.

Griffith seemed to find that declaration significant. "Ghosts are always rather fearsome in Welsh legends." A note of caution hung in his words.

"An enemy?" Miss Castleton spoke in an anguished whisper.

"Miss Castleton." Nickolas stood beside her, Dafydd on her other side, Griffith watching all three of them. "I am not concerned, and therefore, I beg you not to be either."

"But I do not wish for anything unpleasant to happen to you." She turned her enormous brown eyes on him.

And Nickolas found himself quite suddenly in accord with his friends. "I assure you nothing untoward will befall me at the hands of this Gwen." Nickolas offered her a smile, which she returned, much to his delight. "I will, however, fall most decidedly into a decline if you do not agree to treat us to a performance on the pianoforte."

Miss Castleton laughed lightly, the same twinkling laugh Nickolas remembered from London, one that had inspired many an ode from her bevy of admirers. He had never written one, not being a poet himself.

Her color a little high, but smiling as Nickolas intended, Miss Castleton made her way to the very fine instrument he'd been pleased to discover upon taking up residence at Tŷ Mynydd. Soon the melodious sounds of some composer or another floated around the drawing room, leaving Nickolas free to berate his friend without fear of further upsetting Miss Castleton.

She seemed to upset easily. He quickly pushed away the uncharitable evaluation.

"Was it entirely necessary to disturb Miss Castleton's peace for the sake of a simple wager?" Nickolas asked.

Dafydd smiled back at him. "You think I am being insistent because of our bet?" Dafydd actually laughed quietly. "I am insistent because what I say is true, Nickolas. Absolutely true."

If not for Dafydd's infectious laugh, Nickolas might have been irrevocably put out with him. He'd taken the joke too far, certainly. But he didn't seem to mean any harm by it.

"What of you, Griffith?" Nickolas asked. "Have you decided to begin believing in ghosts? Or are you and Dafydd coconspirators as I guessed yesterday?"

"He and I spoke earlier this evening," Griffith said. "He makes a convincing argument."

Had everyone in the house lost their minds?

Nickolas shook his head and made his way to an empty chair. What a wearying twenty-four hours he'd passed. First the uproar of the night before, then Mr. Castleton's vigorous report of all he'd apparently experienced in *her* room, as every single guest, even those who did not believe a word of the legend, had come to call it. According to Mr. Castleton, a gusty wind had blown around the room all the remainder of the night, sweeping all of his daughter's gowns into a pile in one corner and tumbling the bed curtains around the bed posts. He'd insisted it was an invigorating experience.

The Castletons had waited with bated breath for the arrival of *that vicar*, as Mrs. Castleton referred to Dafydd, so they might learn more about the specter that seemed so interested in their family. Nickolas found the entire thing exhausting. If he hadn't been entirely positive that Miss Castleton was precisely the lady for him, he might not have been so patient with her flutterings.

A rustling of papers accompanied the abrupt stop to the notes Miss Castleton had been expertly producing. Nickolas glanced toward the pianoforte. Sheets of music flew off the instrument in all directions.

Miss Castleton hopped up and ran directly to Dafydd, something Nickolas did not particularly appreciate. Her hands clutched his arm. "What have I done to upset her? Does Gwen not like Bach?"

At the instrument the wind continued, growing stronger and swirling more compactly above the keys. Nickolas felt himself tense and his stomach clench. What could have caused such a strange phenomenon? He refused to think of anything supernatural.

Dafydd passed Miss Castleton to her mother's embrace, his own eyes glued to the pianoforte, along with every other pair in the room. Then amidst the flying papers and whipping wind, notes began to play, slowly at first but picking up speed until Nickolas realized a tune was being plunked out.

Mr. Davis recognized it first and quite unexpectedly began to sing. The words were Welsh.

"That's an old Welsh battle anthem," Dafydd whispered. "One which takes great pride in proclaiming war on the English and predicting their painful and inevitable demise." He gave Nickolas a significant look. "She has declared war."

Griffith soon joined his father, singing with gusto. Dafydd took up the tune as well, along with the remaining members of the Davis family. Finally, even the footmen threw in their voices. Nickolas had often heard that the Welsh were excellent singers, and he now believed it, even if he did not particularly appreciate the performance.

As the notes from the pianoforte died away, the remaining papers floated to the floor, and the wind all but extinguished. Just as Nickolas was racking his brain for a reasonable explanation of what he'd just witnessed, his eyes popped.

A lady quite suddenly appeared directly in front of him.

Nickolas stared, unable to speak or move, quite at a loss to reconcile what he was seeing with his own convictions on the supernatural. She was pale and translucent and just as Miss Castleton had said the previous day: *shimmery.*

"Oh, lud," Nickolas whispered. This was not at all what he had anticipated.

Apparently, Mrs. Castleton had not expected it either. She slumped to the floor in a very ungraceful swoon. Everyone seemed too riveted to the scene playing out to pay her much mind.

The shimmery woman spoke then. Nickolas had absolutely no idea what she said, since she quite obviously spoke in Welsh.

Griffith laughed outright, something Nickolas had heard him do only a handful of times in the many years he'd known the generally quiet gentleman. Dafydd simply grinned.

"There are ladies present, Gwen," Dafydd said. "Ladies who understand Welsh. Perhaps you might consider modulating your speech."

Gwen? Dafydd had called her that. Quite calmly. Quite unaffectedly. Nickolas shook his head to dislodge the sudden suspicion that appeared there. He'd never been one to believe in apparitions but could not discount what he was seeing, what they *all* were seeing.

"You are Gwen?" Nickolas heard himself ask and recognized the stunned disbelief in his tone.

"You are English," she snapped back as though it were a dire insult to point out as much.

Nickolas opened his mouth to reply, but the words died unspoken. She stalked toward him, a whipping wind kicking up in her wake. Something in her countenance made him excruciatingly nervous.

"No one goes into my room." She spoke in a harsh and nerve-rattling whisper. "It will be empty tonight, or *you* will bear the consequences."

So chilling was her tone that Nickolas could do naught but nod mutely.

"Mark my words, Englishman. None of your countrymen have yet driven a Welshman from this stronghold, and you will not be the first." With a fierce gust, she disappeared. Vanished.

"Dafydd." Nickolas still stared at the spot she had only just vacated.

"Yes, my friend?" He sounded disturbingly like he was laughing.

"How many blankets do you suppose I need?"

"Blankets?"

"I have a feeling it is deucedly cold in The Tower."

Dafydd laughed harder after that. Once their wager had been explained, the rest of the room laughed as well. The unexpected but undeniable appearance of a woman with no need to actually stand upon the floor—she spent their entire conversation hovering at least six inches above the Turkish carpet—who was not entirely opaque, seemed to have convinced all the skeptics in the room.

"Famous!" Mr. Castleton exclaimed. "Capital!"

Miss Castleton finally managed to rouse her mother. The Davises were excitedly discussing the events of the evening. Dafydd smiled quite smugly.

"You seemed less surprised than the rest of us." Nickolas raised an eyebrow.

"I told you she would make an appearance. It was only a matter of time."

"You've seen her before." Nickolas suddenly realized it was true.

"I grew up in the area." Dafydd clearly thought Nickolas should have made the connection on his own. "I have known Gwen all my life."

"And has she always been so fierce?" Nickolas had not liked the encounter.

Dafydd pondered a moment. "Gwen is a rather complicated ghost."

What an odd statement that would seem taken out of context.

"I have known her to gently sing a baby to sleep, but I have also seen her reduce a grown man to tears of sheer terror." Dafydd spoke in utter sincerity, not a hint of exaggeration in his tone. "If she likes a person, Gwen can be a staunch ally. However, should one displease her, she can make that person's life a nightmare."

"Perfect. She already hates me."

Dafydd actually laughed, and despite his discomfort, Nickolas couldn't hold back a smile of his own. "I suggest you think of a way to win her over."

Nickolas rubbed his chin as if in thought. "Do ghosts like chocolates? Flowers, perhaps?"

"This ghost values only one thing—her bedchamber."

"I should put it to rights, then? And see that she is not disturbed there?" Nickolas already knew the answer to his question.

Dafydd nodded. "Without delay."

"Do you plan to make me fulfill my debt this very night?" He felt a little of his good humor returning. Embracing the existence of the Tŷ Mynydd ghost wasn't coming easily, but Dafydd's infectious laugh was easing the knot in Nickolas's stomach.

"'Tis raining," Dafydd said. "And I cannot guarantee The Tower doesn't leak. Perhaps another night. You can spend this one undoing some of the trouble you have caused."

By the time the party broke up for the evening, Nickolas was less convinced of what he'd seen. His more logical side waged war with the report of his senses. Never mind that eight other people had witnessed the phenomenon as well. Never mind that he could not yet get the rousing, menacing tune they'd sung out of his mind. Nickolas attempted to convince himself that he'd somehow imagined the entire thing or that it had been a joke of some sort, no doubt orchestrated by Dafydd.

Intent on proving the accuracy of his skepticism, Nickolas sent away his valet halfway through his nightly ritual and, pulling his dressing gown over his shirt and breeches, made his way toward the now-empty white bedchamber with a candle in hand. Miss Castleton had been moved to another room, one far less pleasingly appointed but where she vowed she would be more comfortable.

Entering the still, white room, Nickolas felt the need to hold his breath. The peaceful feeling he'd enjoyed on his first visit to the room had been missing during the short interval during which Miss Castleton had occupied it. The realization bothered him. He felt almost as though he'd desecrated it somehow by allowing someone to stay there. Mrs. Baines had implied just that beforehand.

Nickolas shook his head. 'Twas a rather absurd notion.

He glanced around the room. Brand-new candles sat in the wall sconces and table candelabras. The maids had reported that all the candles had gone missing, something Mrs. Baines seemed to think was to be expected. Nickolas lit a few candles, enough to better see his surroundings.

The curtains had been rehung. The floor was free of clutter. The bed curtains, however, remained knotted. That seemed odd. Why hadn't that been seen to? Such a sight felt almost blasphemous.

Nickolas set his candlestick on the bedside table and set to work undoing the damage that everyone credited to the ghost, Gwen. The knots weren't tight, simply plentiful. Nickolas worked for some time at untying the curtains, moving to each corner, finding unexpected satisfaction in putting the room completely to rights.

"Why are you here?"

Nickolas spun around. He hadn't heard anyone enter. The voice was deeply accented but did not sound like any of the maids, the housekeeper, or Mrs. or Miss Davis, though the cadence was unmistakably Welsh. His heart seemed to screech to a halt when his eyes settled on the speaker.

Gwen.

She stood in the middle of the room, no menacing wind, no threatening demeanor. She looked genuinely confused. And shockingly beautiful, considering she was nearly transparent. Her face was pale, made even more so by the bright white of her gown. Her long, flowing hair was decidedly red. He could not recall ever seeing a more striking face, her features symmetrical and classical. He had not noticed that the last time he'd seen her. The fact that she was a ghost had rather distracted him.

"I told you my room was supposed to be empty." A tiny breeze picked up in the room. Somehow, Nickolas knew that meant she was upset.

"I was merely checking to see if the room had been restored." That was patently untrue. He'd come to prove to himself that *she* didn't exist.

"I specifically asked that it be restored *and* emptied." Her look could not have been more pointed.

"You do not approve of me being here, I see."

"I am not certain I approve of you *at all*."

"And what can I do to rectify that?" He did not like the way the curtains rustled in the growing wind.

"You can do nothing," she answered matter-of-factly. "My approval is my own to bestow."

"I have, somehow, in the space of three weeks, having never actually spoken to you, proven unworthy of your esteem?" Nickolas smiled at the irony, willing her to share his humor.

She spoke at length in Welsh as she had earlier that evening. When she finished, Gwen looked at him expectantly.

"I am afraid I understood not a single word of that," Nickolas reminded her.

"You"—she skewered him with a look that sent shivers down his spine—"are not Welsh."

It was a statement of condemnation, Nickolas could tell—the same gripe she'd cited before. His shortcomings had been summed up in four words. It was his parentage and his monolingualism that were responsible for her disapproval of him. That seemed a little harsh.

"My ancestors must have been Welsh, mustn't they?" Nickolas asked. "Else I would not be here."

"The English have been here before," was the reply. "They are not to be trusted."

"That is a rather all-encompassing evaluation. Are you sure it is warranted?"

"Are you sure it is not?"

An unexpected reply, to be sure. Any retort that might have risen to Nickolas's lips died unspoken. A mirror hung not far from where he stood, and in it, he could clearly make out his reflection and a great deal of the room. Staring, Nickolas moved closer. According to the mirror, which he couldn't imagine would lie to him, he stood alone in the white bedchamber.

Nickolas snapped his head back. Gwen still floated in the midst of the room, watching him with narrowed eyes.

Again, he studied the image in the mirror. Though he could clearly see the exact spot in the room where she stood, his mysterious companion made no reflection in the mirror.

Good heavens! He really was talking to a ghost.

"Why are you in my house?" Nickolas asked. Suddenly, her presence was unnerving. He could feel his heart rate increase.

"On the contrary, Mr. Pritchard," she answered, "you are in *my* home."

Chapter Eight

"I SUPPOSE YOURS *is* THE prior claim," Nickolas admitted with a shrug. *I really am talking to a ghost*, he thought, no less amazed than he'd been during their previous encounter.

She actually seemed to smile the slightest bit at his rejoinder. "I have been here four hundred nineteen years. Can you top that?"

"I didn't want to bring it up, but I *do* look young for my age." He actually smiled a little.

Gwen looked doubtful.

"Do you think I could pass for four hundred years old?" he asked.

"Do you think *I* could?"

He immediately shook his head. "No." She appeared young—quite young, actually.

She seemed to like his answer. The tension in her face appeared to lessen, and her eyes softened. 'Twas strange how even translucent features could be readable.

"You are very much like Padrig," Gwen said quite unexpectedly.

"And who is Padrig?"

"He was a son of this house," Gwen answered, "and your several-greats grandfather—the one who hied himself to England. If he'd stayed put we all would have been spared the degradation of seeing Tŷ Mynydd fall into the hands of an Englishman."

He arranged his features in a look of theatrical disapproval. "Those blasted English."

"Words I have uttered many times," Gwen said.

Nickolas actually chuckled. Something about her affronted attitude was no longer menacing but almost petulant, not unlike a child stamping her foot in frustration.

"So is my similarity to this ancestor of mine a positive thing or a negative thing?"

"Both," she answered sharply. "He too was fond of turning anything and everything into a joke, as if there was something to laugh about in every situation. It could be excessively frustrating."

"Strange. I have often been told it is excessively charming."

She did not bother to hide her disbelief. "Is everything a joke to you?"

"I assure you, it is not. Though I have adopted as my life philosophy that 'tis better to laugh than to cry."

She actually smiled, though only slightly. "Padrig once said he'd rather shed tears of laughter than tears of sorrow."

"A wise man, obviously. No doubt he gave rise to extremely wise offspring."

"If he did, I have yet to meet any of them."

Somehow, Nickolas knew a laugh hid under her sharp words. "You disliked him so much, then?"

"I did not dislike him."

"Why is that?" Perhaps he could discover the key to changing her opinion of him if he knew how his ancestor had won her over.

"He was intelligent and well behaved."

There had to be more to it than that. "And . . ." Nickolas prodded.

"And"—she tossed her head of ghostly red hair—"he was far more enjoyable a companion than most of his contemporaries." It sounded as if the words were being ripped from her involuntarily.

"Because he tended to laugh rather than rant and rave."

"That might have had something to do with it." She noticeably fought the admission.

"Am *I* an enjoyable companion?" Nickolas asked, one of his famous smiles slipping across his face. "What with my tendency to laugh and all?"

She seemed even more put out with him than before. Why he enjoyed ruffling her feathers, Nickolas couldn't say. The breeze in the room picked up again, and Nickolas thought it time to change topics.

"You'll notice that Miss Castleton has been relocated," he said. "You have your room back again."

"Except you are still in it," she snapped back.

Nickolas chuckled, though he probably ought to have been worried. He'd been warned not to earn her ire. Everyone else seemed to think such a thing inexcusably foolhardy. He had a suspicion, though he couldn't say where the conviction came from, that Gwen was more inclined to be quiet and unobtrusive than the legend would suggest. He couldn't help thinking that she became fearsome more out of necessity than character.

Something about his unplanned laughter brought a change in Gwen's countenance. Her eyes lost their snapping pride and became infinitesimally pleading. "Your claim to the rest of the house, despite my longer residence, supersedes my own. You have ownership of everything else. But this room is mine. It is *mine*. And I want it back."

"Promise you won't vandalize the place again?" Nickolas asked, teasing her further.

"I would not have done any of that if you hadn't forced me to."

"I forced you to tie your own bed curtains in knots?" He laughed in amused disbelief.

"Mrs. Baines told you to leave my room empty, but you wouldn't. When Miss Castleton first requested to be moved, you talked her into staying. You forced me to run her out." The curtains snapped in a sudden, angry wind.

Run her out. That was the phrase that did it. Gwen had scared Miss Castleton—quite a bit, actually. Nickolas ought to have thought of that slightly sooner, but he'd been distracted. With the memory once again in the forefront of his mind, he found himself growing upset with the vexing specter. "Was it necessary to upset my guest so much?" he asked, feeling the tension inside growing.

"It would not have been if you had acted reasonably. Any of the former owners of Tŷ Mynydd would have seen the error of their ways far sooner than you have."

So now the whole mess was *his* fault? *He* hadn't made a mess of the bedchamber. *He* hadn't put on that ridiculous display around the pianoforte. *He* hadn't gone about the house nearly knocking people over in gusts of ill-directed anger. And to question his suitability to be master of his own home? It was the outside of enough.

"Regardless of your opinion of my suitability, I am the current master of Tŷ Mynydd. You would do well to resign yourself to that fact."

His curt tone had no noticeable impact on her. If anything, she grew cold and authoritative once more. "You would do well, Nickolas Pritchard, to ask around the neighborhood before declaring which of us must accommodate the other. You will find that four hundred years of history is against your chances of pushing me in any direction I do not choose to go."

"Were you this much trouble when you were alive?" Nickolas asked almost bitingly.

"Only when I had to be," she answered, quite on her dignity.

"Then it's a wonder anyone mourned your passing."

With that parting shot, Nickolas left, jaw tight, shoulders tense, marching all the way to his own room. He tossed himself down into a chair near his bedroom window, feeling oddly spent, as though he'd just gone several rounds with Gentleman Jackson.

The late Mr. Prichard had seen fit to warn him of Gwen "at the last possible minute" but hadn't given him nearly enough information. "Tŷ Mynydd is haunted," was the extent of the message. "Tŷ Mynydd is haunted by a troublesome ghost who will be a constant headache to you and will make you uneasy, though not in a way at all connected to her ghostliness, and make you wonder about her long after you've left her presence." That would have been a much more accurate warning.

Why was she so attached to that blasted room? How could she appear so fearsome one moment and almost vulnerable the next? How had she died? How old had she been when she died? And why did he want to know so deuced much?

Nickolas rose irritably, which was odd for someone of his easygoing disposition. He crossed to the window, glancing out over the moonlit grounds of his new home. A gentle breeze ruffled distant trees, and the moon lent a soft glow to the view. Nickolas took several long breaths, feeling the tension slip from him once more.

Tŷ Mynydd was working its magic on him again. Somehow this house, these lands, that he'd never before seen had become as intrinsically a part of him as his own name. Almost as if something in him had been longing to be at Tŷ Mynydd *again*, even though he'd never been there before.

Nickolas chuckled silently. He might even enjoy the night he would be spending in The Tower. It was an intriguing piece of the landscape: a piece of history, a mystery. Something about it grabbed one's attention whenever it was in sight, like it was calling out, asking to be explored.

As his thoughts turned to The Tower, so did Nickolas's eyes. It was visible far to his right, less so than from *her* room but still within sight. Nickolas stared at what he saw. At the top of The Tower glowed a low, unusual light, like a single candle had been lit deep inside, but there weren't shadows that flickered and danced as one would expect with a flame.

He stood watching the odd phenomenon for a few moments, noticing the light change intensity without any distinguishable pattern.

"Odd."

He searched his mind for an explanation but found none. His experiences earlier that evening led him to seriously distrust his own logic. He'd been certain there was no ghost in his home, but now knew there was. He felt there must be a reasonable explanation for the light in The Tower but couldn't help wondering if there truly was. He suspected Gwen had something to do with it. She, he felt certain, was going to cause him no end of trouble.

* * *

It's a wonder anyone mourned your passing.

It was a shame, really, that ghosts were unable to cry. Gwen felt she could do with a prolonged bout of tears. *Mourned* her passing? Indeed not. The entire castle had celebrated. They had turned immediately to their battle plans, and their only thoughts for her were the occasional expression of amazement that she'd had the good grace to depart this mortal coil in such a timely fashion, thereby "consecrating" their efforts. And being not nearly as departed as she could have hoped, Gwen had been handed the distasteful chore of listening to their painful observations.

Her father had seemed a little unhappy, though not to the degree she would have wished. Uncle Dilwyn had seemed infinitely uncomfortable during the entire interlude. While she had always wished he'd shown a little more natural courage, she had appreciated that he, at least, had recognized the near inhumanity of it all.

It's a wonder anyone mourned your passing.

"Touché, Mr. Pritchard," Gwen whispered. Somehow during the past four centuries, she'd spent her time wondering why *no one* seemed to have mourned her passing. It seemed she'd taken the wrong approach.

She'd been a great deal of trouble at times, Gwen knew as much. From birth, she'd caused her father a vast degree of consternation. First came the fact that she had been female when he had been looking for a son and heir. Then, once he'd resigned himself to the fact that she was all he'd have by way of offspring, she'd tried very hard to be the courageous, resilient child he'd hoped for. It had never been enough. And when she'd come of age, something that happened at a much younger age in those days, there had been an absolute dearth of suitors.

Though he'd been unable to marry her to advantage, Gwen had at last served her purpose. She'd saved Y Castell by having the grace to cease living when the time came. Heaven help her, she'd fought for that opportunity to do a good turn for her father. She'd loved him despite him not reciprocating her feelings. She'd spent all of her twenty years unsuccessfully attempting to please him. In the end, she'd had little choice, finding herself, quite against her will, serving as the battle cry of the defenders of her home and destined to wander all alone through its corridors with no end to her residency in sight.

She'd cherished those times when the occupants of Tŷ Mynydd were kind to her. She'd helped raise many of the children who'd grown up to be masters of the house. She'd made friends of many of their wives. And she'd outlasted them all. She had watched hundreds of friends grow old and die and had grieved for each of them. But no one, as Mr. Nickolas Pritchard so succinctly pointed out, had ever grieved for her.

Gwen's eyes swung to the window and inevitably settled on The Tower. It was glowing as it always did when she was upset. Gwen hated it, hated that even her pain seemed to be celebrated as her passing had been so many years ago. She forced her mind to think of happier things, of the joy of a sunrise, of the very room in which she stood.

The glow outside lessened as she knew it would. But her mastery over her emotions did not last long. Even as she thought of those things that brought her some degree of happiness, she couldn't help being reminded of the fact that she enjoyed all of those things entirely, completely alone.

And that no one mourned her.

Gwen turned away from the window, unwilling to actually look at the evidence of her own suffering. She floated silently to the bed curtains, now hanging gracefully unknotted from the bedposts. She'd told the maids to leave them as they were, intending to think of a way to force Mr. Pritchard to undo the mischief as a form of penance.

He'd done so entirely on his own and hadn't seemed the least put out by it. Even her favorite of Tŷ Mynydd's owners hadn't been so generous and lacking in self-consequence. Gwen found herself liking him all the more for it. Therein lay the difficulty. She was growing attached, connected, while he found her simply troublesome.

She'd always known how to deal with each of the masters of Tŷ Mynydd. But Nickolas Pritchard was a mystery. Part of her wanted to make his life a little miserable, and part of her hoped he would prove something of a friend.

She simply wasn't sure which part would come out the victor.

Chapter Nine

NICKOLAS PRITCHARD HAD ADOPTED THE odd habit of bowing to Gwen whenever she happened to cross his path. She could detect nothing mocking in the gesture; it was almost as though he bowed out of civility. Not since her death had anyone treated her like any other young lady.

In acknowledgment of the unforeseen kindness, Gwen decided not to torture the newest owner of Tŷ Mynydd. Yet. His houseguests were generally well behaved. Dafydd seemed to like him. Griffith Davis, the quiet Welshman with intelligent eyes, seemed to like him as well. These were all points in his favor. And though she'd made quite a show of disapproval, Gwen rather liked that Nickolas Pritchard possessed a keen sense of humor. She too preferred to laugh than cry, though she'd had precious little reason for laughter over the past four centuries.

She slid through the outer wall into the sanctuary of her room. Nickolas had been true to his word—she no longer had to share her bedchamber with any of the houseguests.

"Gobs! Do that again!"

Mr. Castleton.

A myriad of creative punishments for Nickolas ran through Gwen's mind as she eyed this latest intruder. She liked him a great deal less than his hen-hearted daughter. Miss Castleton still looked alarmingly faint whenever they encountered one another. As much as she disliked having to reassure skittish people of her entirely innocuous intentions, Gwen found Mr. Castleton's fascination with her unendurable.

"Mr. Castleton." She attempted to keep her tone civil.

"You came right through the walls."

"I am aware of that, sir," she said.

"Do it again."

"I would rather not, actually. Now, good day to you, sir."

"You aren't leaving, are you?" He appeared alarmed at the possibility.

"*I* am not leaving. You are."

He shook his head. "I haven't any plans for the day."

"For the day?" She did not at all like that particular phrase.

Unfettered enthusiasm entered the eyes of her unwanted guest. "Is there anything you can't pass through? Metals? Wood? Churchyards?"

"Why on earth would I not be able to pass through a churchyard?"

"'Tis hallowed ground," he answered as if the explanation ought to have been obvious.

"I am not a demon, Mr. Castleton." How utterly inane.

"You are not an *evil* spirit, then?"

Gwen could not tell if Mr. Castleton found the realization relieving or disappointing. "If I were an evil spirit, would the vicar be on a first-name basis with me?"

"I suppose not." The man very nearly grumbled. "But you are a spirit, are you not? Even if you aren't evil?"

"Would you prefer that I were evil?"

He shook his head adamantly.

"Well, I am pleased to oblige you in that. Now if you will kindly leave me be—"

"How do you pass through the walls as you did?"

Civility did not seem likely to convince him to leave. A greater degree of persuasion seemed called for.

"I pass through it simply by choosing not to knock it down." She put a bit of ominousness into her words.

He remained unconcerned. "You could knock it down?"

"Easily."

"Fascinating."

Good heavens. Subtlety did not seem likely to work on the overly thick man either.

"I do not approve of anyone entering this room without my express permission, Mr. Castleton." She whipped up an impressive wind. The threat of an indoor storm had convinced the man's daughter to leave well enough alone. "I have been known to punish such presumptuousness quite severely."

His eyes opened wide. For just a moment, Gwen thought she'd won the day. Then he opened his mouth and ruined the entire thing. "Can all ghosts create wind like that? Amazing. Utterly amazing."

"I demand that you leave."

He crossed to the wall through which she'd entered and thumped on the stone. "Entirely solid," he said, apparently to himself.

"Do not force me to take drastic measures."

Mr. Castleton addressed her once more. "The wall is solid, but you are not."

"Figured that out on your own, did you?" she muttered under her breath.

"Is there a trick to it?" he asked. "Or does it simply happen?"

"Out."

Any sane person would have fled the room at the icy tone she'd produced. Mr. Castleton obviously did not fall into that category.

"Yes, let's. There is a large metal door on one of the outbuildings. I should like to see you float through that."

"Saints preserve us." Gwen swung about and made directly for the door to the room. She did not bother blowing the door open but passed directly through to the other side.

Mr. Castleton oohed and ahhed and, of course, followed her down the corridor. The man would not be distracted.

He threw out a great many impertinent questions as they made their way toward the public rooms. Gwen chose to ignore every single one of them. Whether or not she slept or ate or was impacted by the weather was no concern of his. The answer, of course, was no on every count, but she kept that information to herself.

She passed into the drawing room but didn't find Nickolas there. Mrs. Castleton sat inside, working at her embroidery. Fortunately for them all, the woman did not see Gwen's arrival. Unlike her husband, Mrs. Castleton didn't find anything fascinating about a ghost. In fact, she looked on the verge of fainting every time Gwen came anywhere near her.

Dafydd sat across the room near the windows, talking with Miss Castleton. Whatever they were discussing seemed to have entirely captured them both. They smiled and laughed a bit. Gwen knew well how much Dafydd had longed for a friend in the years since his return from Cambridge. She was pleased he had found one in Nickolas. If he'd formed a friendly connection with Miss Castleton as well, she would not begrudge him that.

She slipped back out of the room without a sound and continued her search for Nickolas. She found him in the library. He and Griffith lounged leisurely in the two leather wingback chairs on either side of the empty fireplace. Both gentlemen rose when she entered—through an inner wall— and bowed quite politely.

"Miss Gwen," Nickolas greeted her.

"I seem to have contracted a disease that your houseguests brought with them from England." She wrinkled her nose in disapproval as she uttered the last word.

Nickolas smiled in amusement. "A disease?"

Mr. Castleton entered in the next moment, not bothering to knock.

Gwen raised an eyebrow but said not a word.

Griffith smiled his understanding as he resumed his seat. Gwen liked him. He was quiet without being a spineless coward.

"Ah," Nickolas said, eying Mr. Castleton but addressing Gwen. "I see. A catching disease, is it?"

"And fatal, I fear."

He chuckled quietly. "Fatal?"

She nodded. "For the disease."

"So you can pass through stone and wood." Mr. Castleton ticked off the materials on his fingers. "Show me the metal now."

"Distract him," Gwen said. "Or I shall be forced to dispose of him."

Nickolas did not seem to entirely believe her threat. When had she lost her fearsome edge? Gwen crossed her arms over her chest and put on her most determined expression.

"I'll see if I can't find something to occupy his time," Nickolas said quietly.

Such easy acquiescence caught her off guard. Far too many of Nickolas's predecessors had required a great deal of convincing to see things her way. Gwen did not think she was an unreasonable person. She merely wished for some basic consideration. Nickolas apparently meant to give it to her.

"Thank you." She heard the surprise in her voice.

His chuckle seemed to indicate that he detected it as well. "You are decidedly welcome, Miss Gwen."

Nickolas turned to his overly curious houseguest. In a conspiratorial whisper, he said, "I understand from local legend that our resident ghost is far more likely to make an appearance at meals if the table is precisely centered in the room."

Mr. Castleton gave his host his undivided attention. "Precisely centered?"

"Might I suggest you find some means of measuring the table's location and making the appropriate adjustments?"

The man nodded and turned to leave.

"It must be *exactly* centered," Nickolas called after him and received a very purposeful nod.

Only after her overgrown puppy left the room did Gwen allow her amusement to show. "*Exactly* centered?"

Nickolas shrugged, not looking the slightest bit guilty. "Achieving perfect symmetry will take hours. He shouldn't bother you the rest of the afternoon."

The newest master of Tŷ Mynydd was proving a pleasant surprise. "I shall enjoy the peace and quiet."

"Do," Nickolas said. "And see if you cannot concoct a few other 'legends' of which we might make Mr. Castleton aware."

"Distractions, you mean."

He did not admit to such a motivation but looked quite theatrically guilty.

"Have you any suggestions?" she asked.

"Perhaps you have a favorite flower, one particularly hard to find."

"Or," Griffith entered the conversation, "legend might hold that you are more likely to slip into a room if no more than one person is present."

Nickolas grinned broadly. "Mr. Castleton would likely avoid the rest of us at all costs. What say you to that bit of deception, Miss Gwen? You would have many people's undying gratitude."

"Why do you call me 'Miss Gwen'?"

Her question clearly surprised him. "Is there something you would rather I call you?"

"Just 'Gwen' will do."

"If that is what you prefer, then Gwen it is."

Quite against her will, she was finding herself inclined to like Nickolas more with each encounter. "Thank you for being so considerate."

"I think you will find, Gwen," he said, "I am a rather likeable fellow, quite willing to be considerate."

His smile upended her more than a little. "And I think you will find that I am not such a horrible addition to your household as you likely first thought."

"Then perhaps we should agree to be friends and not enemies."

The possibility was appealing. "I should like that."

He gave her another of his excellently executed bows. "Until dinnertime."

"Dinnertime?"

Nickolas gave her a very ironic look. "I believe we will have a perfectly centered table, Gwen. You are required to appear."

"On the contrary," she said. "The table will likely be ever so slightly off center. I am afraid such a thing will be far too disconcerting. I shall be forced to flee, much to my lasting regret."

He chuckled. "I shall explain to Mr. Castleton, though I fear you will quite disappoint him. He will simply have to apply himself to being more precise tomorrow."

She nodded and smiled and left the room, more pleased with her situation than she had been in some time.

Chapter Ten

HAVING A GHOST LURKING ABOUT the place was not nearly as bad, nor as odd, as Nickolas would have expected. He'd grown very quickly accustomed to the situation. And, he'd discovered, he rather liked his resident apparition.

"Quite the house party this is turning out to be," he said, retaking his seat facing Griffith.

Griffith nodded. "Soon ghosts will be all the rage at *ton* gatherings."

Nickolas smiled at the idea. "And perfectly centered tables as well."

"You do seem to be taking the week's discovery in stride, having to admit the house is haunted and all."

Nickolas relaxed his posture, sliding low in the chair and leaning back lazily. "Gwen has been surprisingly easy to accept. She doesn't even seem like a ghost, really, except for walking through walls and hovering above the ground and being translucent."

"Other than that." Griffith smiled a little, shaking his head.

Outside the windows, a breeze rustled the trees. The sky was a deep, clear blue above the rolling green hills. Tŷ Mynydd boasted a view Nickolas felt he'd never grow tired of. Yes, he had certainly done well for himself.

"You realize Gwen is unlikely to be a quiet member of this household, do you not?" Griffith commented after a long, easy silence between them.

Nickolas wasn't overly concerned. "I spent six months when I was twelve living with an elderly distant cousin who was so controlling that every piece of clothing I wore had to be approved by her, right down to my underthings. And at meals, I was required to match her bite for bite. If I survived that, I can certainly put up with a dictatorial ghost."

Griffith's expression turned ponderous.

"Empty your budget, Griff. What's on your mind now?"

"I was only thinking that Miss Castleton seems very..." Griffith's brow furrowed more deeply. "Gwen makes Miss Castleton very uncomfortable still."

Nickolas had noticed that. "She'll grow used to having a ghost hovering about."

Griffith didn't appear confident.

"It has only been a few days, after all. Miss Castleton will rise to the occasion."

Griffith offered no agreement or argument. He took a short sip from his glass of sherry.

Nickolas knew the slight twist of Griffith's mouth for what it was. His friend thought he was being thickheaded.

"You disapprove of my chosen lady?"

"Not at all." That he didn't hesitate was reassuring. "She has a good heart, is of a pleasant disposition. I don't doubt you'd be happy together."

"Then why the warnings over Gwen?"

Griffith never had been one to rush into answers. He took his time as usual. "Miss Castleton doesn't strike me as one with a never-ending supply of hidden fortitude. Gwen, however, does. That might be an uncomfortable combination for the two of them, let alone *you*."

Nickolas allowed that possible complication to settle in his mind. "Let us hope, then, that either Miss Castleton will find her footing as mistress of the house, should things work out for the best, or Gwen will be well-mannered enough, when the time comes, to defer to her."

"And if neither proves the case?"

Nickolas allowed a mischievous smile. "Then my wife and I will simply have to come live with you."

Amusement lit Griffith's eyes. "The both of you? In my tiny bachelor's flat?"

Nickolas shrugged. "It would be cozy."

A quick knock sounded on the door. Dafydd stepped inside, looking excessively pleased with himself.

"What has you so happy?" Nickolas asked. "Did someone donate new prayer books to the parish?"

Dafydd crossed to the fireplace. "My joy is of a far more secular nature than that."

Nickolas exchanged looks with Griffith. He knew his friend wouldn't offer the inquiry hovering in both of their minds, so he posed it himself.

"And that joy would be . . . ?"

"The weather is fine. The sky is clear."

Griffith's smile turned more than a touch dubious. Nickolas, too, didn't believe a word Dafydd said.

"Cut line, Dafydd. The real reason, if you please."

Dafydd tossed something to Nickolas. He caught it easily, though it was longer than he'd expected, at least a foot long. He'd spent enough years unable to afford a personal servant to recognize the spoon-like piece of carved bone immediately.

"A boot horn?" He held the simple contraption up, unsure why his friend had brought him such a thing.

"For getting your boots back on in the morning. After all, your valet won't be spending the night in The Tower."

Dafydd's gleeful references to the weather a moment earlier suddenly made sense.

"With the rain at last gone, you feel I should fulfill the forfeiture of our wager; is that it?"

Dafydd only smiled.

"Very well. What do you say, Griff? Want to spend a night in the menacing ruins of an old tower?"

Dafydd immediately objected. "The terms of the wager didn't include taking someone with you to hold your hand."

"The ghosts in The Tower are that frightening, are they?" Nickolas thought he'd already proven his ability to keep calm in the company of the ethereal.

Dafydd spoke as he poured himself a bit of sherry. "No one knows for certain if there are ghosts in The Tower. I've never heard of anyone actually going inside. Gwen doesn't even do so."

"And you think I'll turn lily-livered?"

"What else should he expect from a *Sais*?" Griffith spoke very matter-of-factly.

Dafydd laughed out loud. "Are Gwen's feelings on the English rubbing off on you, Griffith?"

Griffith answered with nothing more than a look of amusement. He and Dafydd had become fast friends with an insatiable appetite for good-naturedly baiting Nickolas.

"Though I have no idea what the word is that you tossed at me, I suspect a gauntlet has just been thrown."

"Does this mean you'll be slumbering in The Tower tonight?" Dafydd asked.

"Indeed." Nickolas rose and made quite a show of striking a brave and confident pose. "And I daresay I'll become a legend for braving the last remaining bits of Y Castell." He made a valiant attempt at reproducing the odd ending sound he'd heard his staff and Dafydd make when saying the ancient name of the place. It was a sound he'd never heard before, let alone knew how to duplicate.

The immediate laughter from his Welsh companions testified to the mess he'd made of their native tongue.

He tried again. "*Castell?*"

The men only laughed harder.

"But I was at least closer, wasn't I?"

Griffith stood and slapped a hand on Nickolas's shoulder. "Don't worry over it too much. Our people discovered long ago that speaking Welsh is simply one of the many things the English can't help but get wrong."

Nickolas held his hands up in surrender. "Pax, you two. I don't stand a chance with both of you siding against me."

As they made their way from the room, Nickolas's mind lingered a moment on the misgivings he felt during his conversation with Griffith. Should Miss Castleton accept his suit, surely she would settle in and grow accustomed to Gwen being about. Though Gwen was fearsome at times, she might also prove more accommodating than initial impressions would lead one to believe.

No. He needn't worry over all that. Besides, he had a few other things on his mind. Not the least of which was the mysterious remains of the ancient castle. Why did no one go inside? Was it truly haunted? And just what, he wondered, would he find when *he* went inside?

Chapter Eleven

"But it is quite chilly this evening," Miss Castleton insisted, looking genuinely unhappy on Nickolas's behalf. She'd voiced so many objections to his fulfilling the demands of the wager that she had begun to repeat herself.

So Nickolas repeated himself as well. "I agreed to the terms of this wager, Miss Castleton. Surely you would not wish me to act in any way dishonorable."

"But it is cold." She turned pleading eyes to Dafydd, as if begging him to allow Nickolas to cry craven.

When with her next breath she voiced that very request, it was all Nickolas could do not to reply rather sharply that he would not do anything so disgraceful as to renege on a wager. Dafydd saved him the trouble.

"Miss Castleton"—he spoke in a voice far more gentle than the one Nickolas had been prepared to use—"your concern does you credit, and I assure you, should the elements conspire to make Mr. Pritchard miserable, he knows full well that I will not consider him dishonorable for postponing the fulfillment of his debt. Indeed, I have complete confidence that he will keep his end of the wager and am not at all concerned over his honor, nor do I fret that he will put his health in peril in order to prove as much to me. There was, after all, no time limit on our wager."

"Then you will not force him to remain out there should the weather turn shocking?"

Dafydd offered Miss Castleton a smile of appreciative understanding. "Certainly not."

Nickolas heard Miss Castleton breathe a sigh of relief. There was something very gratifying about having his well-being take on such importance for the object of his matrimonial ambitions. Feeling once more quite in harmony with the world, Nickolas made his departure as dramatically as a soldier off to war and, with his valet following in his wake, made his way out to The Tower.

Despite being early October, the night was not overly chilly. Oddly enough, in that moment, he appreciated spending much of his adult life pockets to let. He'd learned to do without the luxuries of life, at times to do without all but the necessities. Sleeping on the floor with a mountain of blankets wouldn't be as bothersome to him as it might be to any number of English gentlemen.

Gramble, Nickolas's valet, followed him silently through the heavy wooden door of The Tower without commenting on the strange situation. They both carried an impressive number of blankets along with Nickolas's personal necessities for the night. Gramble's proper servant's demeanor never cracked, as if his employer were doing nothing out of the ordinary.

The air was colder inside The Tower, owing, no doubt, to the fact that the arrow slits that constituted the only windows in the room had never been filled in with stained glass as so many others had in castles across the kingdom. The room was a circle, the monotony of stone walls and floor unbroken by decorations or furniture of any kind. No doors led off, and Nickolas realized quickly that this level of The Tower was only one room. An upward spiraling staircase was the only way out other than the door that led outside. He wondered if there were any rooms above or if it was purely a battle fortification consisting of nothing but landings on level with more arrow slits and exits to connecting walls that no longer stood.

Nickolas set his armload of blankets down, and Gramble did the same.

"Do you require anything else, sir?" Gramble looked as though he doubted anything could possibly make the situation civilized.

"No, Gramble. Thank you."

Gramble bowed and left, not voicing a single objection nor even looking as though he thought Nickolas ought to back out. That was relieving after Miss Castleton's very vocal insistence that he simply forget he'd given his word.

Nickolas took a walking tour of the small, empty room, which required all of a few seconds. With a shrug, Nickolas returned to the pile of blankets he and Gramble had brought over and began laying out his bed for the night. Two folded blankets made a soft enough mattress for a single night; the others would keep him warm. All in all, not a bad arrangement.

He had several candles he'd been obliged to place on the floor as there was no other surface on which they could be left. Despite the rustic arrangements, he could see. He would be warm. His bed was not too hard.

Nickolas lowered himself to his makeshift bed and pulled off his neckcloth, looking around and imagining the people who long ago must have slept here just as he did. No doubt many of those who'd defended Y Castell during the time of Dafydd's legend had spent their nights here, preparing for battle.

Then his thoughts turned to Gwen. She too would have traversed these walls, walked this floor. It was part of the original castle and the home she would have known during her lifetime.

Once his temper had cooled—that his temper had flared at all still astounded him—Nickolas had come to regret the harsh words he had flung at her when he'd departed her room a few short days earlier. *It's a wonder anyone mourned your passing.* It was a spiteful and hurtful thing to say to any person. She hadn't deserved it, and he shouldn't have said it.

He'd wanted to apologize but had been loathe to bring up the unkind words during their otherwise enjoyable discussion that afternoon. If she'd forgiven him for his words, he didn't want to ruin that by reminding her how horrible he'd been to her.

He pulled off his house slippers, having forgone his tall boots. Even with Dafydd's boot horn, Nickolas could not have easily taken his boots off without Gramble's assistance.

A pair of woolen socks proved just the thing to keep his feet warm, as Mrs. Baines had told him earlier that evening. She really was a gem of a housekeeper. Despite her obvious opinion that he was sometimes overly thick, Mrs. Baines seemed to have a degree of respect for him. They were mutually fond of one another in a way that seemed to combine their roles as employer and employee with that of a prickly aunt and mischievous nephew.

"We none of us go near that Tower unless we have to," she'd further told him. "There's something not quite right about it. Draws a person toward it but not in a pleasant way. Almost like . . . like . . ."

"A siren song?" Nickolas had quickly realized the reference was not one Mrs. Baines was capable of identifying.

"Just you be careful, Mr. Pritchard," she'd said. "Even Gwen avoids that Tower."

Why is that? Nickolas looked around the innocuous room. Other than being a bit cold, The Tower seemed rather ordinary.

Dafydd said The Tower was rumored to be haunted. But while a few people seemed a little afraid of Gwen, no one avoided the house because of her presence. There was a mystery here; he could feel it.

In that moment, Gwen herself floated into the room through the thick stone wall. Despite having come to terms with her existence, her tendency to simply appear had the unfortunate ability to unsettle him.

"Good evening, Gwen." Nickolas managed to make the words seem excessively calm and commonplace.

"Mr. Pritchard," she answered, a certain anxiety in her tone.

"You might as well call me Nickolas. No doubt you have known enough Mr. Pritchards to make the name confusing, otherwise."

"But you are the only one with a *T*," she answered.

"Something, I understand, my branch of the family is only barely forgiven for doing."

"It is something of a desecration." She even smiled a little.

"As much as my being English?" *Her conversation is nothing if not diverting.* It had been at every encounter.

"As you pointed out, Mr. Pr—Nickolas—you are at least partially Welsh. I suppose if we ignore the part which is not, you will eventually prove acceptable."

There was enough laughter in her voice to soften the impact of her words.

"So is there a Welsh word for *bedroll*?" Nickolas asked, straightening the blankets that would eventually serve that role for him.

"You are, then, planning to remain here throughout the night?"

Not another female questioning his honor! A gentleman simply did not back out of a wager. Could they not understand that?

"Indeed, Gwen," he answered rather frostily.

"No need to get yourself in high dudgeon, Nickolas," came the swift rejoinder. "I realize this is all part of some ridiculous bet between yourself and Dafydd. I simply hoped I had misheard the terms."

"I will spend the night here," Nickolas confirmed. "Dafydd would not have backed out if he had lost."

"How long are you required to remain here?" She seemed to grow more nervous with each passing moment.

"Until morning," Nickolas replied, wondering at her agitation.

"Until dawn?"

"I suppose."

"Then I beg of you, please, leave at the very first rays." Her agitation became more apparent. "This is not . . . it isn't—"

"What in the world is that?" Nickolas inadvertently cut off her words when he caught sight of a dim glow emanating from somewhere above the stairwell. It instantly put him in mind of the light he'd seen in The Tower's upper windows a few nights before.

He heard something like a dismayed moan from Gwen. Nickolas's eyes flew back to her. Her focus was on the stairwell as his had been.

"What is it?" He instinctively felt that she knew.

"Is there no other way to fulfill your wager?" She sounded almost desperate on his behalf, still looking unblinkingly up the stairs.

Nickolas shook his head, not feeling offended as he had momentarily been after Miss Castleton questioned his fulfilling his debt. Gwen seemed to understand how a true gentleman lived his life. He did wonder at the reason for Gwen's objection.

She looked back at him, and Nickolas saw something in her eyes he hadn't been expecting: fear. She who had the maids quaking was afraid of something. If he didn't miss his mark, it was something up those stairs.

"This is a dark place, Nickolas," she said pleadingly. "Horrible things have happened here. It will eat away at you, fill you with cold and darkness. Do not stay any longer than you must."

Normally, Nickolas would have laughed at such a dramatic speech, but the look in her eyes, the pain so evident in her face, lent her words a degree of conviction that completely erased any sense of theatricality.

"What sort of horrible things?"

Gwen closed her eyes, shaking her head repeatedly. The glow up the stairs increased in intensity.

"There is something up there." He moved toward the stairs.

"Nickolas, don't."

"I saw The Tower glowing a few nights ago," he said as he took the first few steps. "I need to know what is causing it."

"Please, Nickolas." She suddenly appeared in front of him. "Stay on the lower level. There is nothing up there but pain."

But curiosity had ever been Nickolas's besetting sin. He pushed on, determined to investigate the source of the odd glow.

Gwen put out a hand as if to hold him back. But not being corporeal, her ghostly hand simply disappeared inside his chest. It was the oddest sensation, almost like warm water trickling slowly inside. The warmth was concentrated, precisely the size of her hand, and didn't spread or radiate.

She pulled her hand back almost the instant it passed through him, her look one of embarrassment and frustration. Gwen even glanced at her hand as if it had somehow failed her. Nickolas looked at her hand as well, missing instantly the warmth it had created. He seemed to be growing colder.

"I wasn't intimidated by all the chaos you caused in the house, Gwen. Going up these stairs to investigate isn't going to overset me."

But she didn't move. Gwen just watched him, concerned and undecided. He knew perfectly well he could simply walk through her—she had inadvertently demonstrated her own less-than-solid state. But that felt tantamount to running the poor lady over. And there was something unnerving about the thought of feeling that deep, concentrated warmth pass completely through him.

"You are determined to go up?" Gwen asked quietly.

"Quite."

"Then I will go with you."

"Do you think I need protection?" Nickolas smiled mischievously.

The tiniest hint of a smile broke the solemnity of her features but just as quickly slipped away. "I imagine you will need someone to drag your lifeless body back down the stairs."

Nickolas started to chuckle but then noticed Gwen didn't appear to be joking.

"Is there someone dangerous up there?" Nickolas asked, suddenly alarmed.

"No. Not *dangerous.*"

It took but a moment to realize what Gwen had implied if not outright told him. "But there is someone up there."

There was someone in The Tower. But who? Who was Gwen protecting, for it certainly seemed that way. He could not have an interloper hiding away on the grounds of Tŷ Mynydd. And despite Gwen's reassurance, Nickolas wasn't convinced the intruder wasn't dangerous. Why else would he be hiding?

Perhaps Gwen wasn't protecting the intruder but protecting *him* from whatever threat was up those stairs.

Nickolas gave her a look of warning so she would have a chance to move or glide or whatever she meant to do to get out of his way. She seemed to understand the unspoken message and began floating up the stairwell, keeping pace with Nickolas. And she didn't seem happy about it.

Higher and higher they climbed. A deep, penetrating cold seeped into Nickolas's body. But the air didn't seem to change, and his breath didn't form clouds in front of him the way it usually did when the air was chilled. This cold was different. Icy fingers wrapped around his chest, squeezing his lungs, making each breath harder to take than the last.

His ascent slowed, and his legs seemed to cramp as cold penetrated his muscles and bones. Around him, the glow grew but brought no warmth.

Gwen remained close to him but with anxiety written on her face.

"Gwen?"

She looked at him, her eyes filled with piercing pain. "This is a horrible place, Nickolas." But she did not hang back, did not abandon him as he continued his climb.

The cold grew with each step. He slowed. Indeed, Nickolas could tell he was hardly making any progress at all. Up ahead, the ethereal glow around them illuminated a door across the landing to which the winding stairs led. The sight of it, for reasons he could not explain, made his heart pound unpleasantly, almost as if he were seeing something imminently threatening.

At least a dozen steps separated him from that door, but Nickolas found he couldn't move any farther. The cold had turned to freezing pain, and his lungs felt near to collapse. He leaned against the side of The Tower. A cold sweat trickled down his forehead.

Gwen hovered just in front of him, blurring his vision of the door he felt pulled toward, even as his conviction that it was best avoided increased. "Please turn back, Nickolas," she said. "You are a good person. This is no place for someone like you."

"What happened here?" He gasped, his lungs still frozen and painful. "Why are you so afraid?"

"It was wrong," she said. "What they did. The spirit of it lingers here still. It's . . . it's evil."

And somehow, that was the right word for it. *Evil.*

"Please turn back," she said again. "You are brave to have come this far. No one else ever has. But please, Nickolas, please go back."

"I'm not sure I can." What possessed him to admit as much, Nickolas couldn't say. Perhaps it was the poignancy of her own candidness.

"Are you unwell?" she asked, genuine concern in her voice.

"It is so cold," he said.

Gwen looked back at the door above them and seemed to shudder as if she felt the cold as much as he did. "You must go back down."

Nickolas agreed, seeing the wisdom in her suggestion, even if he did not understand the logic. He could not say why it was so cold at the top of the stairs, but he'd been warmer, less crippled on the ground level. He needed to get back there.

One step at a time, he climbed back down, the warmth in his body returning only slightly. He staggered once, and Gwen, seemingly automatically, reached out to help him, only to pull her arms back when she recognized her own inability to offer aid. Again that look of embarrassed frustration crossed Gwen's face.

Nickolas was still shivering as his feet reached the lower level of The Tower. He staggered to his bedroll, dropping onto the folded blankets, exhausted. Something was very wrong at the top of The Tower. He pitied whoever Gwen believed resided up there. Those thoughts were, however, fleeting. He was too cold, and his lungs hurt too much for meditating on what had happened.

A quick, sudden wind blew his pile of blankets over him, bringing a modicum of warmth back to his body.

"Thank you, Gwen," he said, curling into a ball like a tiny child.

"Please don't go back up there," Gwen whispered.

"I don't plan to."

She sat on the floor beside him, to the extent a ghost can sit—it was something of a hover in a seated position.

"Do you promise me you won't go up?"

He looked across at her, struck by the tears he heard in her voice. Her eyes darted back toward the stairwell, which still glowed ominously. Such stark fear and anguish filled her expression. If he weren't frozen to the core, he'd have reached out to her. Then again, he could not have actually touched her.

Nickolas pulled the blankets up more tightly around his neck, praying the painful chill would ease. "Afraid you'll have to come claim my lifeless body?" He tried to joke despite his chattering teeth and the continued oppressive influence of his trip up those stairs.

"Please don't joke about that." Her tone was so small, so pained, he couldn't bring himself to tease any longer.

"I won't go up again," he told her. "In fact, I plan to avoid this place entirely."

The tiniest of smiles touched her face, an obvious show of relief. "That is wise. I avoid it myself."

"You need not have come, Gwen."

"Few people have come here over the centuries," she said. "I have never allowed any of them to do so alone. No one should ever have to be here alone. Not ever."

Though he could not say precisely in what way, he knew that statement was significant. Gwen's history was tied to this place. She refused to force any person to remain in its walls alone, and he would, so long as he was master of Tŷ Mynydd, see to it that she was never again forced to enter The Tower.

Chapter Twelve

"Nickolas."

It was a soft, distant whisper. Sleep began its slow retreat. Nickolas opened his eyes a sliver. He saw a face that he vaguely knew had haunted his dreams, though he couldn't quite place the delicate features. Of its own volition, his hand reached out to touch the face he couldn't tear his half-asleep eyes away from.

He cupped his hand to caress her cheek, but his fingers met nothing but soft, warm air as they slipped into the translucent absence of flesh.

"Gwen." He whispered his sudden understanding.

Her eyes dropped in seeming embarrassment. Nickolas pulled his hand back, feeling unexpectedly disappointed. He sat up and looked around, only just beginning to remember where he was: the bottom of The Tower, under a pile of blankets.

"It is dawn," Gwen said quietly. "You should go now."

"You were here all night," Nickolas muttered in amazement.

Gwen had been noticeably disturbed by their abbreviated climb up the stairs. Long after Nickolas had regained his warmth under his pile of blankets but had not yet settled into sleep, Gwen continued to "sit" on the ground near him, anxiety written on every feature of her face. Her eyes had shifted repeatedly to the glowing stairwell.

Her suffering had been obvious, but she had, it seemed, remained there throughout the dark, quiet hours of night while he slept. Almost like she'd been guarding him the way she was supposed to have guarded her home from attack all those centuries ago.

"It is time to go," Gwen insisted, just as a knock on the heavy wooden door leading outside echoed around the room.

"Nickolas?" Dafydd's laughing voice barely penetrated the door. "Did you make it?"

Nickolas pulled himself to his feet and made his way to the door. He was wrinkled from head to toe, his hair, no doubt, hopelessly mussed. He pulled open the door, secretly enjoying the shock his appearance would probably give.

Dafydd, however, simply laughed. "That bad, was it?"

Griffith, standing there as well, grinned in obvious amusement.

Nickolas managed to summon a smile he didn't particularly feel. "I'll be glad to be back in my own bed."

"We'll give you a hand with your blankets." Dafydd stepped inside but froze only a few feet from the doorway.

Nickolas followed Dafydd's eyes to where Gwen floated, watching them.

"Have you been in here too?" Dafydd asked her.

She nodded. "This is not a good place, Dafydd. He ought not to have been required to be here."

Dafydd crossed to Gwen, the concern on his face obvious. "But you never come to The Tower."

She returned his gaze, eyebrows knit, still looking anxious. "He should not have been here alone," was the almost inaudible reply.

Dafydd studied her more closely. "It really is as bad as you say, then?"

"It is far worse than any of you could possibly guess." She seemed to pull herself together again. "Now help him gather his things so he can leave."

Somehow, Nickolas didn't feel it was a curt dismissal but rather further evidence that Gwen, who many described as fearsome and who had more than once come across as prickly, was concerned for his well-being.

Silently, they grabbed the pile of blankets and Nickolas's discarded personal effects and made their way to the door.

"Dafydd." Gwen's voice met them before they left.

They all looked back.

"No more wagers involving The Tower." Her gaze shifted from him to both Nickolas and Griffith. "From any of you."

Dafydd smiled empathetically and nodded. Griffith added his silent agreement. Somehow, Nickolas knew Gwen didn't need his consent. He had no intention of ever coming back to that place, nor would he force anyone else to do so.

They began their walk back toward the house. A rush of wind passed them. Nickolas knew it was Gwen fleeing The Tower.

"If I had known our wager would mean Gwen would force herself to spend the night in The Tower, I would have chosen a different forfeiture," Dafydd said with something like a sigh in his tone.

"She was decidedly unhappy there."

"I have never known her to spend any time in The Tower," Dafydd said. "She has always given it a very wide berth. When I was a child, even, she would not permit any of the local children to play in it or near it. Some she resorted to frightening away from it, despite the fact that she strongly objects to frightening children."

"That is a very strong dislike of the place," Griffith said. "Not one to be taken lightly."

"And entirely warranted," Nickolas said wearily. He remembered all too well the chilling pain he'd experienced on the stairwell, remembered the fear in Gwen's eyes, the sense of near doom he himself had felt.

Dafydd, Nickolas realized, was watching him closely, a look of concern and curiosity on his face. "Did something happen there last night, Nickolas?"

Griffith's gaze had locked on him as well.

He did not, at first, answer. How could he possibly explain what he'd felt? How did one convey that sort of inexplicable experience?

"Do either of you believe in evil spirits?" It was an abrupt opening to the subject, but he could not think of another way of beginning.

Only a fleeting look gave away Dafydd's surprise. "The Bible certainly makes mention of demons and evil spirits."

Leave it to a clergyman to set one's mind at ease by means of holy writ. "Not that kind of spirit." Nickolas smiled at the relief he felt when Dafydd didn't immediately dismiss his question or laugh outright. "I mean, do you believe that . . . that a place can have a spirit, a *feeling*, about it?"

"As in, a chapel feeling peaceful?"

"I suppose." Nickolas shrugged. "Except, a . . . a . . . *bad* feeling."

Griffith entered the discussion. "I have heard soldiers recounting how the site of a past battle can have an unsettling feel about it."

"Have you ever known a place to have an evil feel?" Nickolas pressed, looking between his two friends.

"Evil?" Griffith seemed to think a moment before shaking his head. He watched Nickolas, a look of anticipation on his features.

Dafydd hadn't answered at all.

Nickolas glanced at him, half expecting a look of dismissal or mockery. But Dafydd seemed more thoughtful than anything else. They were nearly to the house. Nickolas wondered if Dafydd meant to answer his question or if he was simply ignoring it. He felt foolish enough having broached the subject. He was beginning to regret it.

"The Tower feels that way?" Dafydd eventually asked.

Nickolas nodded. "The feeling grows as one ascends the stairs."

Again, Dafydd fell silent, his feelings, for once, hidden behind an unreadable mask. Griffith looked as confused as Nickolas felt.

Two footmen met them at the door, taking the blankets from them. Just as Nickolas lifted a foot to step inside, Dafydd stopped him with a hand on his arm. "You need to see something."

* * *

"The middle of nowhere," Nickolas answered after Dafydd asked him if he knew where they were.

Dafydd laughed, but looking around, Nickolas couldn't help thinking he'd given a rather apt description. The three of them had walked to the north property line of Tŷ Mynydd and stopped at what looked to Nickolas to be a place of absolutely no significance.

"Until approximately three hundred years ago, this was the path of a road that ran along the Tŷ Mynydd property line. A second road crossed this one only a few yards from where we are now."

Nickolas nodded his understanding, assuming there was another reason they'd come to that particular spot besides a discussion of centuries-old roads.

"I can see you think I am absolutely daft to have brought you here." Dafydd chuckled.

"*Are* you daft?" Griffith asked.

Dafydd shook his head but didn't look the least offended. "You are horribly lacking in faith, my friends."

"Then perhaps you should take pity on our lack of confidence in you and simply explain your reasoning," Nickolas said.

Dafydd began walking, motioning for the others to follow him. After only a few steps, the air around them changed. An oppressive coldness seemed to trickle in, not unlike what he'd felt on the first few steps of The Tower. Nickolas instinctively slowed his pace. Griffith did the same, shooting him a look of confused inquiry.

"There." Dafydd pointed ahead to a large rock, easily the size of a sow.

Etched deeply into its surface were words, worn with age but clearly visible.

Griffith muttered a shocked exclamation, his eyes on the inscription.

Nickolas couldn't make out the words. "I don't read Welsh," he reminded them both.

Dafydd undertook the translation. "It says, 'Here lie the remains of Arwyn ap Bedwyr, buried at these crossroads. Be ye chastised and warned all ye who disregard the laws of God.'"

The seeping coldness had not lessened but had rather increased as they'd come closer to what Nickolas now knew was a burial site. He rubbed at his arms as he looked warily at the large stone. "What did Arwyn ap Bedwyr do that deserved such a scathing epitaph?"

"Do you not know what a burial at a crossroads means?" Dafydd gave him a pointed look, and Nickolas instantly began searching his memory.

Griffith pieced it together first.

"A suicide."

"Precisely, though most crossroads burials are unmarked. This one is unique in that respect."

According to Dafydd's description, this now wild and untamed corner of the estate had once been very public. "He was made an example of?"

Dafydd nodded. "His suicide rocked the tiny community surrounding Y Castell. Arwyn ap Bedwyr, you must understand, was the local priest."

The priest? Nickolas felt his eyes pop. He didn't think he'd ever heard of a priest committing suicide.

"Some believed that having been a man of God, he would be spared the disgrace of a suicide's burial. That obviously was not the case. And it was rumored he was guilty of some horrific misdeed. The only other man who knew of his guilt, whom locals believed had been a coconspirator of sorts, died only a few short weeks before Arwyn's death."

"Was this other man's death a suicide as well?" Griffith asked.

Dafydd shook his head. "The other man's health had begun a steep decline in the preceding years. The impact of his overwhelming guilt, many said. Arwyn, unable to die naturally as his comrade had, took his life to escape the pain, leaving others to deal with the aftermath of both his original wrongdoing and his community-shaking suicide."

Griffith moved closer to the rock. "Was it the suicide or his rumored misdeed that inspired this scathing inscription?"

"I don't know. Perhaps both."

The quiet peace of the landscape stood in sharp contrast to the unsettling feel of the place. As he stood listening to Dafydd's explanation, Nickolas fought against a growing urge to flee with all possible haste. Griffith looked every bit as unsettled.

"And the priest's history is why this place feels so . . . so . . . ?" He searched for the right word but came up empty.

"Bad?" Dafydd finished for him, using Nickolas's own inadequate wording from earlier. He nodded, however, indicating that was the case. "Less than a century after Arwyn's death, the roads that crossed here were rerouted. There were a great many complaints about the *feeling* here, as you described it. Travelers disliked the arctic sensation. Horses were known to spook. Many acknowledged the horrible feeling of the place. The fact that you describe The Tower as feeling the same way makes me wonder if the two are connected somehow."

"That both were the sites of suicides?" Griffith suggested.

"No," Dafydd said. "Arwyn ap Bedwyr was the priest at the time of the Welsh uprising. He would have been there at the time of Gwen's death and the subsequent battles. The fact that Gwen is—and, it seems, always has been—afraid of going inside The Tower would, to me, indicate that she knows something about it that the rest of us do not, something that happened during her lifetime."

Nickolas nodded. "That 'something' could be the reason for the spirit of the place."

"And since this unexplained incident she seems to know about and Arwyn ap Bedwyr's unknown crime are rumored to have occurred during that same period, one must wonder if those two events are . . ."

"Related," Griffith finished the sentence.

Dafydd nodded. "If not one and the same."

"It is possible, I suppose," Nickolas said.

"Consider this," Dafydd said. "Arwyn's rumored coconspirator was none other than Cadoc ap Richard, Gwen's father. And toward the end of Gwen's life, Gwen's father had a falling out with his brother, Dilwyn, over something neither would disclose, and the two never reconciled. They had, until that time, been quite close."

"There is a mystery here," Nickolas muttered, his mind beginning to spin with the possibilities.

Griffith had never been one to let a puzzle go unsolved. His expressive face clearly showed he'd begun pondering the mystery as well.

Dafydd nodded and indicated they ought to begin their return trek to the house. The cold had seeped into Nickolas's very organs, and he did not wish to remain.

They walked in silence. Nickolas was deep in thought, as, he assumed, the others were. Questions raced through his mind.

What could those men have done that was horrible enough for the priest to have taken his own life out of apparent guilt?

Was there truly a connection to The Tower?

Was there a connection to Gwen?

Words she had said to him the night before flew into his thoughts.

"Gwen talked about this last night," Nickolas blurted.

"What?" Dafydd spoke with a mixture of surprise and eager astonishment.

"I am certain of it now. She said, 'What they did was wrong. And the spirit of it lingers here still.' *Here* meaning The Tower."

Dafydd shook his head as if in disbelief. "How did you force that revelation out of her?"

"I didn't *force* anything." He quickly realized Dafydd was not accusing him of anything.

"Gwen never—*never*—talks about her life or the people she knew then or the things she saw. It is rather remarkable that she even hinted at her past."

"She spoke of it as something of a warning," Nickolas said.

"Like the warning she issued all of us over future wagers?" Griffith asked.

Nickolas nodded. "She meant to convince me to never return."

"Perhaps, despite her dramatic first appearance, Gwen has come to care about what happens to you." Griffith looked to Dafydd for confirmation, as did Nickolas.

"Perhaps," Dafydd said with a shrug.

"Or," Nickolas threw in, "perhaps she was afraid she wouldn't be able to finish me off herself if she left me to the not-so-tender mercies of whatever specter resides at the top of The Tower." Nickolas shook his head and couldn't prevent himself from chuckling. Gwen had, many times since their first introduction, glared at him as though she'd like nothing better than to toss him out of the house.

"You do not know her well, then," Dafydd said. "She's not nearly as troublesome as you seem to think she is."

A screech carried over the short distance between the three men and the house. Visible in several of the windows were people moving in what seemed to be chaotic patterns. Several windows stood open and sounds of pandemonium flooded out.

"That sounded decidedly 'troublesome' to me," Griffith said.

Nickolas raised an eyebrow at both men before they all sped their steps.

"What has she done now?" Dafydd mumbled.

Chapter Thirteen

GWEN KNEW SHE OUGHT NOT to have lost her temper so entirely. In her defense, she'd had a very long, trying night. And Mr. Castleton was barely tolerable under the best of circumstances.

Every room in the old wing of the house would have to be put to rights. Her spurt of temper had sent a wind of tornadic proportions down the corridor, blowing open doors and wreaking havoc in all of the chambers. Instead of running in panic, Mr. Castleton had simply stared all the more pointedly and whispered an awe-filled "Fascinating."

Only when the butler, housekeeper, most of the chambermaids, and two footmen had come into the room searching for the source of the disturbance had she been able to rid herself of him.

"Remove this man from my room, or this very house will fall down around you."

As always, they took her threat seriously. She would never actually level Tŷ Mynydd. Although, heaven knew, she'd tried to do precisely that to The Tower, only to discover that the protection she offered her ancestral estate applied very pointedly to that most hated part of it. It simply couldn't be brought down. Neither wind, nor hammers, nor workmen could pry a single stone from its walls, let alone bring it crashing to the ground as ought to be done.

"What mischief is this, Gwen?" Nickolas unexpectedly appeared from the doorway behind her.

Gwen spun around to face him. His presence made her breath catch in her chest, despite the fact that she did not actually breathe.

"Was it your intention to give the staff extra work with this fit of yours?"

Any hopes of empathy and understanding from the man she had given up her very peace of mind to protect the night before disappeared with those words. Only a monumental effort prevented her from knocking him literally off his feet with a repeat performance of her earlier indoor whirlwind.

"At least you have managed not to tie your bed curtains in knots." Nickolas crossed to her bed and fingered the perfectly hanging curtains.

"*He* was in my room," Gwen said between clenched teeth.

"*He?*" A twinkle of amusement lit Nickolas's eyes.

He thought this funny, did he? Found her suffering entertaining? He certainly wasn't the first over the centuries, but it was somehow harder coming from him.

"I told you my room was to be empty. I told you it was *mine*. Mine!" Despite her intentions, a stiff breeze picked up again.

"Do you plan to tell me who it was that invaded your bedchamber, Miss Gwen, or shall I simply have every male in the household drawn and quartered?" He produced that smile she knew meant he was joking with her. She was determined not to be amused.

"Mr. Castleton."

"Ah." A look of sympathy passed over his smiling countenance, and Gwen felt the tiniest bit better. "He invaded your sanctuary?"

What little comfort he'd given her a moment earlier vanished at his tone. "There is no need to mock me, Nickolas Pritchard. All I have asked of you is this room. That is all I have ever asked of anyone." Her voice rose with each word, her emotions coming painfully to the surface. She turned away from him, willing herself to remain in control. "Everything else has been taken away from me. Everything! And you mock me for clinging to this tiny comfort."

"Oh, Gwen." His voice grew suddenly gentle. She felt her defenses begin to crumble. "I did not intend to mock you. I have often been told I have an atrocious sense of timing when it comes to teasing remarks."

"In my day, a jester could have his head cut off for 'bad timing.'"

A smile lurked in Nickolas's eyes. "That is a very good way to run out of jesters."

"And heads," Gwen added.

He chuckled, and the sound warmed her. He had a way of calming and soothing her, even in moments of distress. She'd never known anyone quite like him.

"I don't think I would have enjoyed being a jester under those conditions," Nickolas said.

"You certainly would have been motivated to practice your teasing more."

"And I begin to think you are in need of practice at *being* teased, Gwen." He sat on the edge of her bed.

"Most everyone is afraid of me." She shrugged. "I suppose it is hard to tease someone who frightens one half to death."

"Perhaps they fear for their heads." He grinned at her.

Gwen hovered closer to him, feeling tired. Weariness was the worst of the *feelings* she had to endure. Ghosts, she had discovered early on, could grow weary but could not sleep. Rest was the closest she came. The previous night had been anything but restful.

"Did anyone tease you before you became a fearsome specter?"

"My father was not really a teasing sort of gentleman."

Nickolas leaned back against one of the posters of her bed, turned so he faced her full on. "Neither was my father."

"I find that hard to believe." Gwen pulled her legs up, hovering in the same cozy position she'd favored as a young girl. "If you did not inherit your sense of the ridiculous from your father, then where did it come from?"

"From my grandfather, according to the stories I have heard." Nickolas's expression grew unmistakably nostalgic. It was a side of his personality she had not yet witnessed. "I have few memories of my mother, but I do remember that she liked to tease and smile and laugh."

Gwen knew well the look that passed through his eyes. "You miss her."

He nodded. "Almost twenty years have passed since she died, and I still miss her every day."

Empathy surged through her at the familiar pain in his voice. "My mother died over four hundred years ago," she said, "and I have never stopped missing her."

"Then she was already gone when you . . ." The sentence dangled unfinished, but she knew what he meant.

"Mother died when I was twelve. Things might have ended differently if she'd still been alive." Gwen had often told herself as much, though she had never been certain. Mother's influence on Father had not been enormous, but she might have softened him.

"What was your mother like?" Nickolas asked. "I find myself picturing her a great deal like you, with red hair and just enough fire in her eyes to make a man think twice about crossing her and, yet, undeniably gentle and softhearted."

His words touched her deeply. "That is very kind of you."

He smiled—how she loved that smile! "I hope you noticed that I was not teasing in the least."

"You really think those things about me?"

"How could I not?"

"You are an unusual sort of gentleman, Nickolas Pritchard." She shook her head in amused surprise. "One would think you thought of me as a real person."

He actually looked confused. "But you *are* real."

A tiny laugh escaped, surprising even her. She never laughed. "Would Mr. Castleton stare at me day in and day out if I were *real*?"

He shrugged. "Mr. Castleton is *also* a rather unusual sort of gentleman."

Another unexpected laugh followed that observation. "I will not argue with you on that point."

"Gads, you're beautiful when you smile like that." Even Nickolas looked a little surprised at his blurted observation.

Feeling a little uncomfortable, Gwen rose and floated away from the bed. No one had ever paid her such a compliment, in life or in death. After a moment's silence between them, Nickolas followed her to the window.

"Is having your room undisturbed important to you, Gwen?"

"I know I am unusually insistent about it, but this has been my sanctuary for four centuries." His sincere expression gave her the courage to continue. "I need it, Nickolas. I need a place where I can be still and undisturbed and . . . peaceful."

He smiled empathetically. "I will ask Mr. Castleton not to return, but I cannot guarantee he will acquiesce. He seems to have developed something of an obsession."

"I know." Gwen sighed. "He has the most disconcerting habit of staring whenever I am nearby."

"Strange," Nickolas said. Gwen recognized his teasing tone, and it made her feel a little less burdened. "One would think that encountering a ghost was not an everyday occurrence."

She fought back a smile. "It *is* an everyday occurrence for me."

Nickolas laughed, just as she knew he would. "Touché."

Many years had passed since she'd lived with someone who made her smile, whose company she enjoyed more often than not. "How do you propose I keep him from staring at me?" Gwen asked, knowing Nickolas would come up with a diverting response.

He made a noise of deep thought and rubbed his chin. "Could you frighten him enough to send him scurrying away every time you come into a room? I understand you are quite good at terrifying people."

"I have tried," Gwen answered dryly. "He finds it 'fascinating.'"

Nickolas shrugged. "They do say love is blind."

Gwen laughed. How she'd missed laughing over the centuries since Padrig had left. He was the last who regularly pulled a chuckle from her. Yet even his company had not been as pleasant as Nickolas's. "The last thing I want is Mr. Castleton to be nursing a *tendre* for my ghostliness."

"Your *ghostliness*." Nickolas laughed all the harder. "You are a treat, Gwen. A treat." Nickolas made to take hold of her hand, seeming to realize the futility of the gesture only after his fingers slipped entirely through hers.

Frustration like she hadn't known since her lifetime slipped over Gwen. Why must she forever be denied the comforting reassurance of a simple touch? She needed it, especially after the night she had spent.

Thoughts of The Tower overtook her mind. She would gladly have endured Mr. Castleton's unnerving stares if it meant she—and Nickolas, at that—could have avoided the night spent in The Tower.

"I am sorry, Gwen. I—"

Gwen just shook her head. "Your wager was only for one night, wasn't it?" She was probably rude for cutting him off, but she needed to know he wouldn't go back. She hated the thought of returning but would not leave him there to endure The Tower alone.

"It was."

Silence hung between them. Gwen attempted to force all thoughts of the night before from her mind, tried to keep herself from reliving the memories that had been forced upon her as she'd sat there hour after hour in a place she utterly abhorred.

"It is a horrible place," Gwen whispered.

"I am beginning to understand that," he answered quietly. "Which makes me wonder all the more why you stayed there last night. As I told you, you didn't have to."

She'd stayed because she couldn't bear the thought of him in such an evil place. She'd worried that he'd try to go up the stairs again and something horrible would happen. She had wanted to protect him, as she did the house and yet, *not at all* as she did the house. Just being near him as he slept had afforded an unexpected amount of satisfaction and pleasure. Her fingers had itched almost unbearably to reach out and touch him.

"I have a feeling, Gwen, that you stayed there for my sake." Nickolas smiled at her, not the laughing, teasing smile she saw so often but a compassionate, understanding, comforting smile. "And I thank you for that."

"You're welcome."

"And thank you for not strangling Mr. Castleton." The twinkle returned to his eyes. "Tempting as I am sure it is. That would certainly put a damper on my first house party."

"I will attempt to restrain myself." Gwen smiled in reply.

"And I will attempt to restrain Mr. Castleton. I think his family would be distraught if he met an untimely end."

"Most families would be." She fought down the reminder that *not all* families mourned the death of a family member. The Castletons did not seem that heartless. "Miss Castleton appears to be a kindhearted young lady."

"She is." Something about the tone of his response made Gwen bristle. "Miss Castleton is universally admired."

Gwen looked more closely at him and instantly wished she hadn't. A certain amount of interest showed in his expression as he spoke about Miss Castleton.

"She is considered quite a diamond, in fact," Nickolas continued. "Well mannered. Good family. Precisely what a gentleman most hopes to find in a lady."

Nickolas looked almost as if he were trying to convince himself of the well-deserved praise he heaped on Miss Castleton. Gwen gave little heed to the seeming contradiction. The list was certainly long enough, and Gwen had no doubt Miss Castleton deserved every accolade. But she had to fight a surge of unexpected emotion: the same feeling that all but consumed her whenever the staff served pheasant at dinner and she was forced to smell it but could not eat it. She felt suddenly, entirely, and inexplicably jealous.

"And she is also quite pretty," Nickolas added.

"Yes. She is." Miss Castleton *was* pretty. And unlike Gwen, Miss Castleton wasn't devoid of color, very nearly transparent, and *not alive*.

Nickolas made another of his deep-in-thought noises, though this time not as theatrically as before. He truly was pondering something. Gwen refused to think about what that something might be.

"Is there anything else I can do for you, Gwen?" Nickolas asked, breaking abruptly from his reverie. "Besides doing my best to dampen Mr. Castleton's enthusiasm."

"If you can accomplish that much, I will be grateful." She floated away from the window and Nickolas, telling herself he had every right to praise Miss Castleton.

"Are you certain?" he asked from behind her. "You seem less enthusiastic than earlier. Has something upset you?"

She couldn't remember the last time someone felt like her concerns, her feelings, her needs were truly important. Such treatment of a ghost was, she supposed, understandable—few people, if any, realized she had feelings and needs despite not having a body—but even in life she'd been pushed aside and disregarded.

Despite his kindhearted inquiry, Gwen couldn't bring herself to tell Nickolas what had upset her. How could she tell him she wished he thought *she* was precisely what he'd always hoped to find in a lady? How could she tell him that she enjoyed their conversations and that this latest reminder that she was a dispensable, overlooked part of the house made her feel even more lonely?

She couldn't.

"No, Nickolas," she answered before sliding through a wall and back outside the house. "There is nothing else you can do for me."

Chapter Fourteen

MRS. CASTLETON ORGANIZED A PICNIC the following afternoon for "the young people." She declared it a fine opportunity for becoming better acquainted. She gave Nickolas explicit instructions to look after her daughter during the outing, though she assured him of her utmost faith in his trustworthiness. She was also sure to add that the presence of a vicar must certainly add to the respectability of the idea.

He, Miss Castleton, Griffith, Alys, and Dafydd were shooed from the house with enthusiasm.

"You said you hoped the house party would provide ample opportunity for furthering your acquaintance with Miss Castleton," Griffith said as they walked in the direction of the chosen meadow. "It seems you are to have your wish."

"In spades," Nickolas added. He'd been granted her company for a walk in the gardens but a few days earlier. Now they were to have a picnic without any true chaperone beyond a vicar who was, himself, young and unmarried.

"Have you discovered Miss Castleton is not to your liking after all?" Griffith asked.

Nickolas shook his head. That was not the issue at all. He liked Miss Castleton as much as he ever had. She'd proven herself every bit as congenial and sweet tempered as he'd believed her to be. "I like her very much indeed."

Griffith made a sound of contemplation, one that had on any number of occasions annoyed Nickolas to no end. That particular sound often preceded an evaluation of what Griffith perceived as his inner thoughts and motivations. Nickolas spared himself the lecture and moved swiftly to help Alys spread out the picnic blanket.

Dafydd had been charged with carrying their meal. He set the large basket on the blanket and opened the top. Miss Castleton knelt down before it, helping pull the various dishes out from inside. It was to be a very informal picnic, without the servants and serving tables one often saw at more impressive outdoor entertainments in the *ton*.

Nickolas took a seat on the blanket and leaned against an obliging tree. Griffith's question repeated in his thoughts. *Have you decided Miss Castleton is not to your liking after all?*

He watched the lady he'd quite particularly invited to the house party as she set out the afternoon's meal. She guided Dafydd in the placement of each dish but did so with a graceful gentility, smiling her gratitude at his help. A more kindhearted lady he would be hard-pressed to find. As he'd told Griffith, he liked Miss Castleton very much. But, he admitted to himself, he'd lost a bit of his enthusiasm for her company.

"Coconut macaroons?" Dafydd asked, pulling yet another dish from the basket.

Miss Castleton nodded. "Mother had them included especially for me. They are my favorite."

Dafydd smiled. "They happen to be my favorite as well."

Nickolas leaned his head back. He needn't worry that Miss Castleton would be neglected. Dafydd knew how to be a gracious neighbor. Though he'd seen a grand amount of food emerge from the large basket Dafydd had lugged to their chosen spot and every guest other than Mr. and Mrs. Davis and Mr. and Mrs. Castleton had come on the outing, Nickolas couldn't shake the feeling that something was missing.

Alys was busy gathering a late-season flower of some sort that Nickolas had seen growing in various spots on the estate. Griffith seemed content to sit quietly, watching clouds wander across the sky. Dafydd and Miss Castleton had the meal nearly all set out. It was, by all accounts, a picturesque arrangement. So what exactly was nagging at him?

He knew the answer in the very next moment. His gaze fell on Gwen, not far in the distance, walking the long-fallen walls of her ancient home. The day felt incomplete because, until that moment, he'd not seen her.

* * *

After the passage of hundreds of years, Gwen no longer found it odd that the unseen walls of the one-time castle still felt solid beneath her feet. She walked them, looking out over the wild and untamed land that surrounded her home. Sometimes she thought of those she'd once known as she wandered about in solitude. That day, however, her thoughts were of the present and the man she had come to care for deeply.

She looked back over her shoulder when she realized the sound of his voice calling out to her wasn't merely her imagination. There he stood, gazing up at her from not many yards away. His smile never failed to warm her heart.

"Good day to you, Nickolas," she answered back.

"Are you on official guard duty just now, or do you have time to come sit with us?"

She looked just beyond him to what appeared to be a small picnic gathering. Gwen hadn't been on a picnic since before the last Mr. Prichard's time as master. He'd been a bachelor his entire adult life, and something of a hermit at that.

Gwen stepped from the spot where the castle wall had once stood and, as she discovered was always the case, slowly floated down to the ground. Nickolas walked toward her, meeting her partway.

"Does this mean you'll join us?" He seemed so very hopeful. She loved that he wished to have her around. Perhaps she wasn't as dispensable to him as she feared.

She eyed the impressive spread of food already laid out on the blanket. "I can't actually eat, you realize."

"Oh, but that was my plan all along. If I invite guests who don't eat, I get to eat their portion."

Gwen smiled at that. "That is a bit devious, Nickolas."

"I believe the word you meant was *ingenious*."

They joined the others at the blanket. While Miss Castleton didn't seem entirely at ease in the presence of a ghost, she no longer grew alarmingly pale.

"Good afternoon, Gwen," she offered, every inch the perfect hostess.

"I hope you do not mind that I've joined you." Gwen knew the appropriate protocol required an invitation.

Miss Castleton dismissed the objection with a simple smile and a soothing word of welcome. *Everything a gentleman wishes for in a lady.* She could see why Nickolas felt that way.

"Besides," Dafydd added, "this picnic is supposed to be for 'all the young people.' We couldn't very well leave you to spend the afternoon with the parental set."

"Never mind that I am several centuries older than anyone in 'the parental set,'" Gwen answered dryly.

The group laughed at that, just as she had intended them to.

Nickolas sat near a plate of sandwiches. Gwen opted to sit nearby but not directly at his side. If he was on the picnic in order to further his suit with Miss Castleton, distance seemed more than called for.

The meal was casual and decidedly friendly. Gwen joined in the conversations, all the while watching the others.

Alys and Griffith behaved just as a sister and brother always seemed to. There was a decided fondness behind their needling of one another. Knowing smiles filled with history counterbalanced the looks of annoyance they occasionally threw at one another. Gwen had been in the company of Alys Davis a few times over the course of the house party and had seldom heard so much as a peep out of her. But her brother managed to pull entire sentences from her.

Gwen missed that feeling of family. A few of Tŷ Mynydd's masters and mistresses had included her in their family circle as something resembling a distant relative. But not since her mother's passing had she truly felt the close connection so obvious between the Davis siblings.

She glanced at Nickolas. He smiled at her.

"Griff used to complain all the time about his 'obnoxious little sister' when we were kids. They do get along better now than they did then."

Apparently, Nickolas had noticed her watching the brother and sister. "I was actually thinking how much they seem to like each other and how nice it must be to have family."

Nickolas's expression turned wistful. "I don't think anyone appreciates the appeal of family as much as those who don't have one."

How perfectly he'd articulated what she felt. She let her eyes wander back to the others. Perhaps they would all accept her into their circle and she need not be quite as alone as she had been over much of the past four hundred years. With Nickolas there, she would once again feel she had someone who cared about her.

"Are those chrysanthemums?" Miss Castleton asked, her gaze traveling off in the distance.

"I honestly have no idea," Nickolas answered.

Gwen had to smile at his ignorance. "They are, indeed, chrysanthemums."

"May I pick some, Mr. Pritchard?" Miss Castleton looked infinitely hopeful.

"If Alys can pilfer my wildflowers, you certainly can."

Alys gave Nickolas a look of annoyance not unlike the ones she'd given her brother. Gwen wondered if Nickolas knew how much his connection to the Davises resembled that of family.

"Will you come with me, Dafydd?" Miss Castleton asked.

Dafydd assured her he would enjoy the outing. He offered her his hand to help her stand. They walked off arm in arm toward the clump of flowers, their conversation friendly and cheerful. Gwen hadn't been jealous of such things in all the years she'd spent as a ghost, but she felt more than a twinge of it then. She would love to walk with her arm in Nickolas's or to simply hold his hand.

"Dafydd and Miss Castleton seem to get along well," Griffith said to no one in particular.

Gwen looked at Nickolas, wondering what he thought of the closeness she saw between the lady he'd told her he greatly admired and his bachelor friend.

"A good thing too." That was not the response Gwen would have expected. Had she read too much into the situation? "It would be terribly awkward if they despised each other."

Griffith popped a macaroon into his mouth and made no further comment. But Gwen saw in his ponderous expression that he was just as puzzled by Nickolas's lack of concern as she was.

Perhaps he was not as serious in his pursuit of Miss Castleton as everyone believed. A bubble of hope grew inside at the thought. Of course, he might simply be convinced Dafydd and the young lady were no more than friends and posed no threat to his courtship of her.

How she hated even thinking of Nickolas and Miss Castleton in those terms. Gwen thought she'd seen in his face, heard in his voice, that he cared for *her*. He sought her out. He smiled when their eyes met from across the room. He treated her with a tenderness she didn't think she'd misinterpreted.

A small voice in her thoughts insisted she was the reason Nickolas no longer paid such pointed attention to his beautiful houseguest. He did still walk around the gardens with Miss Castleton, and they were often thrown together in the evenings after dinner. But Gwen hadn't seen the same fondness in his eyes that had once been there when he looked at Miss Castleton.

Rather, she thought she saw it when he looked at *her*.

She held back a small smile. Perhaps, with him there, she would no longer be so entirely alone.

Chapter Fifteen

"And how are we to be entertained tonight?" Nickolas pulled Mrs. Davis aside upon entering the drawing room after dinner several nights after his sojourn in The Tower. "You have been very tight-lipped about your plans, I will have you know."

She smiled mischievously. He'd seen that exact expression on Griffith's face more times than he could even remember when they were lads—and always before they'd undertaken some ill-formed scheme or another. "As soon as we are all assembled," Mrs. Davis said.

Nickolas glanced around the room.

Mr. and Mrs. Castleton sat near the pianoforte. Alys and her father were in conversation beside the fireplace. Griffith had taken up a book. Dafydd and Miss Castleton appeared to be enjoying a lighthearted conversation.

"Are you waiting on Gwen, then?" Nickolas asked.

"Indeed."

A moment later, Gwen floated into the room looking decidedly uncomfortable but determined just the same.

"Miss Gwenllian." Mrs. Davis greeted her first. Nickolas couldn't say Gwen's proper given name, no matter how hard he tried. Mrs. Davis had no difficulty, despite not being a native speaker of that difficult tongue.

Gwen smiled at their hostess, and Nickolas was struck by the beauty of that gesture. He had always considered Gwen beautiful, despite her pallor—she could not help that, after all—but her smile stole his breath.

"I received your note," Gwen said to Mrs. Davis.

"I hope I was not too presumptuous," Mrs. Davis answered.

"Not at all."

Nickolas very nearly laughed out loud when he considered the absurdity of the situation when viewed from an outside perspective. They were all conversing quite naturally with a ghost. He'd never have believed it possible only a few short days earlier.

"I have had an absolutely wonderful idea for the final days of this gathering and wish all of your input," Mrs. Davis announced to the room.

She had everyone's attention.

"The last day of October is *Nos Galan Gaeaf*, and I believe we ought to hold a gathering of sorts. A small festival, if you will."

"*Nos Galan Gaeaf?*" Nickolas asked, the words as unfamiliar as nearly every other Welsh phrase.

"The last day of the year, according to the ancient calendar," Dafydd explained. "The celebration is a very old folk tradition."

Nickolas knew Dafydd was fond of tradition and proud of his Welsh heritage, so why did the suggestion seem to make him uneasy? Indeed, his eyes kept darting to Gwen, a look of nervous anticipation on his face.

Gwen's look proved far more worrisome. Nickolas recognized the spark in her eyes even before he noted the breeze ruffling his guests' hair. He held his breath, ready to intervene.

"I am to be your *Ladi Wen*, then?" Gwen asked, her voice tight with an emotive mixture of anger and offense.

What, Nickolas asked himself, was a "*Ladi Wen*"? He looked between Dafydd, who appeared a little offended as well, and Griffith, who seemed as confused as Nickolas.

Gwen's expression grew ever more mutinous. "Do you wish me to pose at a stile? Or perhaps the entrance to a footpath would serve better." The wind kicked up with each tense word Gwen spoke. "You could invite the local children to make a game of trying to spot the fearsome *Ladi Wen* and provide them with all the salt they could wish for to toss at me and in my path."

"Miss Gwenllian," Mrs. Davis replied, her tone extremely patient and empathetic. Nickolas felt the tension begin to dissipate. It didn't seem Mrs. Davis had meant the insult Gwen and Dafydd had apparently felt in her suggestion. "I asked you to attend this discussion specifically so that I might assure you I had not intended any such thing. I would not, *could* not, be so callous as to make a mockery of your existence."

Gwen nodded. "I apologize, then, for my baseless conclusion." The low wind in the room died down in that instant, and Gwen retreated from the group, perching near a window. What was it, Nickolas wondered, that drew Gwen to windows? Every time he came upon her, it seemed, she was gazing out a window.

"For the sake of our English friends," Mr. Davis entered the conversation, "perhaps it would be wise, dear, to explain a few of the Welsh customs. This way, they will be better able to decide which would be most enjoyable to include."

"In that, I think we may appeal to Mr. Evans." Mrs. Davis turned to look at the vicar. "He knows his folk traditions well, I daresay, and would know which are observed in this area of the country."

"I do, indeed." Dafydd looked one last time at Gwen before taking up the task handed him. "*Nos Galan Gaeaf*, celebrated on the last day of October, marks the start of the new year in the ancient Welsh calendar. It also signals the beginning of winter. On *Nos Galan Gaeaf*, the spirits of the dead are said to walk the earth, and the division between this world and the next is believed to blur. Many traditions emerged as a result of this night when ghosts roam freely. The spreading and carrying of salt and other preserving agents, as Gwen referenced. Special attention is paid to anointing stiles and footpaths with these agents, as that is where the ghosts are apparently most likely to appear."

"And what is *Ladi Wen*?" Nickolas asked.

"'*Y Ladi Wen*,'" Griffith said, managing a tone of mystery. "The White Lady—said to either be the bringer of treasure or a terrifying ghost, depending on where in the country the legend is being told."

The White Lady. No wonder Gwen assumed she was meant to play that role. Her ghostly attire was entirely white.

"And in addition to *Y Ladi Wen*," Dafydd continued, "is *Yr Hwch ddu gwta*."

That was certainly a mouthful. "I am not even going to attempt to say that one," Nickolas said. "I'm still working on Y Castell."

Every Welshman in the room winced.

"It could not have been *that* bad," Nickolas insisted.

Griffith leaned in closer and, in an exaggeratedly loud whisper, said, "You should probably just call it 'the castle' and skip the Welsh altogether."

Nickolas took the ribbing in stride. "What is this other creature you mentioned?"

"The tail-less black sow," Dafydd said.

"A *sow*?" Nickolas smiled. "And does the pig bring treasure like the White Lady supposedly does?"

Griffith shook his head. "The black sow has the disconcerting tendency to eat any individual unfortunate enough to encounter it. And it has a decided preference for the taste of young children."

Nickolas laughed in both shock and amusement. "It is a wonder Welsh children ever sleep at night with such tales rolling about in their minds."

"The thirty-first of October is a night given to revelry and merriment, despite its darker associations," Dafydd assured him. "Various games involving apples are common, as are fortune-telling and bonfires."

"It sounds a great deal like All Hallows' Eve." Mrs. Castleton echoed Nickolas's thoughts. "Though the fearsome sow was unexpected."

Unexpected? Nickolas smiled to himself. One never knew what Mrs. Castleton would say next.

"I don't know that I like the idea of horrible ghosts or fortune-telling," Miss Castleton threw in her impression.

Nickolas opened his mouth to reassure her but was prevented by Mrs. Davis retaking control of the discussion.

"We would not be including fortune-telling in our celebration," she told the younger lady. "And other than our own Gwen, who is most certainly not horrible, ours will not be a *ghostly* entertainment."

Nickolas looked to Gwen, wondering how she would respond to the compliment she had just been paid. She still gazed with apparent interest at the completely darkened view out the window.

"There wouldn't be any other ghosts?" Mr. Castleton asked, obvious disappointment in his tone.

"No, sir," Mrs. Davis said.

"Don't you have any friends you could bring along?" Mr. Castleton's question was directed at Gwen.

Her head snapped in his direction, the fire in her eyes again, and Nickolas knew instinctively it was time to intervene, lest Mr. Castleton not be around to enjoy the festivities they were planning.

"Tŷ Mynydd has a vast apple orchard," Nickolas said to the room. "We should have plenty of apples for any and all games of which your imaginations can conceive. And I do not think dancing would be amiss either. Indeed, there must be a few families in the area who could be prevailed upon to attend." He glanced at Dafydd during the final sentence, knowing the vicar would know more of the area than he himself did.

"Indeed," was Dafydd's response. Where was the man's usual enthusiasm? Why did he continually gaze at Gwen? Was there more about the proposition likely to be upsetting to that lady than the original worry that she herself was to serve as a form of entertainment?

"Wonderful," Mrs. Davis said. "If you will compose a list of appropriate families, I am certain the Castleton ladies would assist Alys and me in writing out the invitations. Though I have one more suggestion."

"And what is that?" Nickolas asked on behalf of the group, forcing himself to reenter the conversation and not think too hard about what was eating at Dafydd and Gwen.

"I believe our small ball would be wondrous as a masquerade," Mrs. Davis said. "A *true* masquerade in which each participant wears a mask along with his or her formal attire. There would be no questionable costumes nor concealing dominos."

Echoes of agreement and growing excitement filled the room. Only a few moments passed before the entire assembly was lost in planning the event, ten days hence. Dafydd had been commandeered by the ladies to help assemble a guest list and offer insight into local customs and opinions on the appropriate decorations.

Mr. Castleton had crossed the room to where Gwen stood, still at the window. Even from a distance, it was obvious he was staring at her again. Feeling the weight of his promise earlier in the week, Nickolas started across the room to pull the man away.

He was, however, waylaid before he reached his destination.

"A *Nos Galan Gaeaf* ball," Mr. Davis said. "You will be the Welshest of Welsh landowners before long if this keeps up."

Nickolas smiled at the irony. "I think your wife is attempting to help me save face with my neighbors by hiding my Englishness as much as possible. I really ought to thank her."

"But not until you are certain she hasn't offended Gwen," Griffith said. "I thought for sure the furniture would topple before Mother had a chance to defend herself. Or at the very least, we'd once again find ourselves an impromptu choir cheerily declaring war on the Saxon invaders."

Mr. Davis laughed heartily. "That was something of an experience, was it not? Being called to arms by a lady who lived at the time of Owain Glyndŵr. Stirs the blood in any Welshman's veins."

Griffith smiled at his father but, turning in Nickolas's direction, rolled his eyes. His father's overabundance of national pride had often been a source of amusement to Griffith, though he had his moments as well.

"If you will excuse me, I'd best go extricate Mr. Castleton before Gwen *spills* the blood in that Englishman's veins."

Chuckles echoed behind him as Nickolas continued his trek across the room.

"There must be someone else you could call on," Mr. Castleton implored, his tone indicating he'd made this request unsuccessfully before. "Someone who might be prevailed upon to make a brief appearance. It is to be a celebration of your kind, after all."

It was the "your kind" that had been the proverbial straw on the camel's back, Nickolas realized later, after Mr. Castleton had been helped back to his feet and the nearby furniture put back to rights. Gwen had disappeared without a sound beyond the gust of wind that had knocked Mr. Castleton onto his exceedingly ample backside. But the look on her face hadn't left Nickolas's mind. She'd been hurt by Mr. Castleton's words. Deeply hurt. And Nickolas felt shaken by it, as if he were to blame for her suffering.

Nickolas walked out with Dafydd when that gentleman was ready to depart for the night. "Do you have a minute tomorrow when you could come to the vicarage?" Dafydd asked as they approached Nickolas's carriage, which was waiting to take him back to that exact location.

"Certainly. I'll head in that direction in the morning."

"Excellent." Dafydd sounded distracted, his expression far off.

"Are you excessively lonely, or is there a reason for my visit?" Nickolas inquired, trying to recapture the lighthearted feel of their earlier association.

Dafydd did smile at that. "There is something I think you need to see. Especially in light of tonight and the upcoming ball."

"In regard to Gwen?"

Dafydd nodded. "Our discussion at the crossroads has stuck with me, has made me think more on what little I know of her."

Nickolas understood that. He had thought a lot about her as well. And wondered about The Tower. About her father. About the fallen priest.

"Shall I extend the invitation to Griffith? He's been puzzling this over as well."

Dafydd nodded and stepped inside the carriage. "I will see you tomorrow, then."

"Tomorrow," Nickolas acknowledged.

He stood there in the courtyard for a moment after the carriage rolled out of view, his mind full. There were too many possibilities to guess at what Dafydd wanted to show him. Nickolas hoped it would shed light on his very mysterious, very permanent houseguest. He'd had his first hint at her inner sadness while climbing the stairs of The Tower. Their conversation the next day had only solidified that impression—she seemed unhappy and lonely, and she'd been playing least in sight since then.

The pain in her eyes that night had been almost palpable. Nickolas desperately wanted to ease that suffering. How he'd wanted to hold her hand only a few days earlier! But there was nothing of flesh and blood about her, thus no way to offer comfort through touch. He could not dry her tears, though thinking back, he wasn't sure she'd shed any. Was that a lack of emotion? Or was she simply unable to?

Movement out of the corner of his eye caught Nickolas's attention. Upward his eyes moved, settling on something white and billowy, floating high above the ground. It was Gwen, walking perfectly level, as if on an invisible wall. Her hair and skirts fluttered furiously in a breeze that did not affect a single nearby tree.

It is said that at night she can be seen walking high above the ground, where the castle walls once stood, standing guard over her home. Dafydd's retelling of Gwen's legend came back to Nickolas's mind. She was walking those walls. Alone.

He watched her a moment longer, his heart growing heavy at the sight of her. More and more, his suspicion that she was lonely took seed in his mind. What must it be like, he wondered, to remain behind when one's loved ones were long since passed away?

He shook his head, feeling helpless and frustrated, and turned to go back inside. If only he could hold her hand in his, offer her the comfort of that simple gesture and words of reassurance. But anything he said would be hollow and pointless.

Nickolas glanced over his shoulder one last time. She continued to walk, though the temperature dropped. Could she feel the cold? he wondered. He hoped not. He hoped that if she did, Gwen would return inside. If only Mr. Castleton would stay out of her room and leave her that single source of comfort.

It might, in fact, be a very good idea to check to make certain no one was invading the sanctuary of Gwen's room.

Chapter Sixteen

"Mr. Castleton." Nickolas ought not to have been surprised to see the man standing eagerly in the middle of Gwen's room. But he'd let himself hope that Mr. Castleton's earlier run-in with Gwen would have sated his appetite for ghostly encounters.

"She enters through the wall," Mr. Castleton informed Nickolas without bothering with any of the civilities that usually accompanied a greeting. "It is amazing to watch. I never tire of it."

"I think, Mr. Castleton, she may tire of having an audience," Nickolas countered as gently as he could manage through his growing frustration. He did not wish to offend the man, simply to send him on his way for the night.

"Nonsense, m' boy." Mr. Castleton turned back toward the room's exterior wall, no doubt anticipating Gwen's return.

Obviously, he needed a new tactic. "With the upcoming ball," Nickolas said, trying to sound convincing, "I think Gwen might be inspecting the ballroom."

Mr. Castleton's eyes grew wide in anticipation.

"Perhaps if you hurry, you can see her slide through a wall or two." The temptation was likely more than the poor gentleman could resist. A moment later, in fact, he scurried from the room.

Nickolas shook his head at the retreating back of their resident ghost chaser. How Mr. Castleton must drive his family mad a great deal of the time. For just a moment, Nickolas actually felt grateful to have no family of his own. If nothing else, that saved him the difficulty of troublesome relations.

Nickolas pulled his set of keys from his jacket pocket, fumbling for a minute before coming across the skeleton key to all the bedchambers. It did not take a great deal of imagination to picture Mr. Castleton hurrying back once he failed to locate Gwen in the ballroom. Nickolas stepped into the doorway, intending to close it behind him and lock Mr. Castleton out, but he stopped with his hand on the doorknob.

He ought to go. He ought to leave Gwen's room empty and quiet, but he wanted to see her, to know that she was well, that whatever had bothered her during the evening's discussion no longer upset her.

Though many found her fearsome and frightening, Nickolas had seen compassion in her that he'd seldom found in others. Hadn't she remained in The Tower with him during his sojourn there despite her own suffering? Hadn't she offered compliments to Miss Castleton despite that young lady's initial, though unintentional, invasion of Gwen's own refuge?

Gwen was the kind of lady any gentleman would admire. Or *had been.* Nickolas wasn't sure precisely how to refer to her, whether the present or the past was the accurate approach. She had lived long ago but was there in his house still.

Whatever the syntax, he did admire her. He came to the sudden but irrefutable realization that he admired Gwen more than any other lady of his acquaintance. They'd spoken at some length in The Tower before exhaustion had overtaken him. It was that conversation, coupled with many others, and his own observations of her and what he'd learned of her from others that had solidified his good opinion of her. But not until that moment, standing alone in her safe harbor, did he realize how much he'd come to care for her.

It was something of a jolt. Although he acknowledged Miss Castleton's good heart and fine looks and recognized that his favored houseguest was a good person at heart, Nickolas could not remember ever thinking as highly of her as he already did of Gwen.

But what good can come of that admiration? Nickolas asked himself. There was no future to be had with a ghost. There could be no happy ending to an attachment with a lady who was already dead.

When Gwen floated into the room by way of an outer wall in the next moment, Nickolas could barely summon a smile, so suddenly depressed were his spirits.

"Nickolas!" she blurted in obvious astonishment at his presence.

"I have sent Mr. Castleton on a mad dash about the house," he managed to say.

"You are very good, Nickolas."

He shrugged. "I cannot help myself."

Another of her brilliant smiles crossed her face. She did not produce them often, but when she did, Nickolas was irresistibly drawn to her. He stepped back inside, closing the door behind him, locking it so Mr. Castleton could not return.

"Your household seems on the verge of utter disruption," Gwen said.

"The festivities, you mean?" He did not attempt to pronounce the name of the Welsh holiday, knowing his accent was atrocious.

"Balls and gatherings have never failed to turn Tŷ Mynydd upside down."

Nickolas leaned against the wall on the opposite side of the window by which she stood. "You've been around for a great many of them, I imagine."

"Four hundred years' worth." Her lips turned up in amusement.

"I've been to a few balls that seemed to last four hundred years."

She laughed. He'd come to truly enjoy that laugh. "I should warn you now: I never make an appearance at balls. I rather despise being put on display, and it always seems such a shame to wreak havoc on an event that requires so much effort and planning."

He shook his head and clicked his tongue. "Yet you made quite an appearance at this house party."

"You deserved that, and you know it—you and your skepticism."

He chuckled. "I certainly saw the error of my ways."

She moved closer, skewering him with a theatrical look of scrutiny. "And you cannot honestly say you aren't secretly pleased that I disrupted your party."

Nickolas shook his head. "You are the best part of this very welcome inheritance of mine."

Her studying look grew less theatrical and more sincere. "Better even than Miss Castleton's parents finally acknowledging your existence?"

"They were certainly within their rights to protect their daughter from a penniless fortune hunter." He'd told himself as much many times.

"You never were any such thing."

Her fierce defense of him made him smile ever more broadly. "But they did not know that."

Gwen crossed her arms in front of her, a pointed look on her face. "Then they could not have taken any time to get to know you. I, for one, think such a thing is utterly inexcusable."

She looked adorably offended on his behalf. He stepped closer to her. "Are you telling me that if you had been confronted with my complete lack of funds, you still would have given me the time of day?"

"You are a wonderful person, Nickolas. No amount of money can buy that."

He had the strongest urge to kiss her. His lungs constricted painfully as he fought to settle his pounding heart. What he wouldn't give to be able to hold her in his arms. It was a helplessly frustrated feeling.

He forced himself to produce a light tone. "Before these compliments go entirely to my head, I'll bid you good night."

"And a good night to you too, Nickolas."

"I will instruct the staff to keep this room locked so Mr. Castleton cannot return to disturb you."

"Thank you," she said, her smile beyond brilliant. Nickolas's heart skipped a beat.

"See you tomorrow, Gwen."

Her smile widened, her eyes shining. *She must have been an unparalleled beauty in her lifetime*, Nickolas thought to himself, stepping out of the room into the corridor and pulling the door closed behind him.

With a click, he slung the deadbolt into place. Nickolas leaned his forehead against the outside of Gwen's door.

"What have I done?" he muttered. He was half in love. With a ghost.

*　*　*

"You look done to a cow's thumb," Dafydd said the next morning.

"Done to a cow's thumb?" Nickolas repeated with a bark of laughter, despite his own heavy heart and mind. "Where did you come across that bit of Town cant?"

Dafydd smiled back. "Do you think no one from Wales has ever been to London?"

"Of course I don't think that. Griff here is quite the man about Town every Season."

Griffith looked appropriately diverted by the blatant untruth. Neither of them had ever been in demand amongst London's elite. "I simply did not realize *you* had been to Town," Nickolas added.

"Many times," Dafydd answered. "I am a Cambridge lad, you know. We wandered down to London now and then."

"I barely finished Eton, I must admit," Nickolas said. "Not for want of intellect, I assure you. For want of blunt. The paltry inheritance left me by my loving but impoverished parents only stretched so far."

Nickolas wasn't sure why he'd admitted that. Griffith, of course, knew the tale from having been present for most of it. But that part of his history was something Nickolas seldom, if ever, spoke of. He'd enjoyed the academic and social aspects of Eton and had at first felt the loss of his university experience acutely. The sting of it had lessened over the years, though he still felt a stab of regret when he thought back on it all.

"Before this delves into tangents completely off topic," Dafydd said, "let's get back to my original observation. You do not look well, Nickolas. Are you?"

"Merely tired," was Nickolas's safe response.

He hadn't slept well, questioning his own feelings as he had through most of the hours he'd spent in his bedchamber. The state of his heart weighed on his mind.

He'd fallen in love with Gwen, with her indomitable spirit, her compassion, her wit and humor. And she was dead. She was even more beyond his reach than Miss Castleton had been before his unexpected inheritance. But he had not, in the days he'd mourned Miss Castleton, felt that loss to the degree he was pained by these realizations about Gwen.

Dafydd seemed to realize there was more Nickolas wasn't divulging but chose not to pry. "Are the two of you up for a short walk?"

"Always," Griffith answered.

"As *short* as the last discovery trek you took us on?" Nickolas forced himself not to dwell on his depressing reflections.

Dafydd smiled. "Not quite so far—just through the churchyard."

Through the churchyard did not prove an entirely accurate statement. Their journey ended only a few yards from the ancient stone chapel, at the base of a small statue depicting an angel, arms crossed at her breast, face turned upward, an expression in her features that spoke not of the usual joy one saw on the faces of stone cherubim but of such stark fear and sadness it took Nickolas's breath away. Like the stone at the crossroads, ancient Welsh words were etched in the statue's base.

"As I doubt you have become literate in Welsh over the past few days, I will translate the inscription," Dafydd said. "Unless Griffith would like to do the honors?"

Griffith shook his head, intent on circling the statue, his perpetual look of pondering on his face.

"The words, more or less, say, 'May our gratitude be as undying as she who unwillingly became our war cry. May her forgiveness be as all-encompassing as her protection.'"

A lump materialized in Nickolas's throat in perfect unison with the formation of a thought in his mind. "This is . . . is Gwen's . . . grave." The words came out choppy and strangled. *Gwen's grave.* His stomach twisted painfully.

"No," Dafydd answered unexpectedly. "She died during the siege of Y Castell. And was not buried in the churchyard. No doubt the looming threat of battle required speed rather than ceremony. This statue was erected some five years after her death. Her remains, however, were never moved into the churchyard."

"Where was she buried?" Nickolas looked once more at the statue. Its expression mirrored almost perfectly a look he'd seen in Gwen's face before: anguish and sadness.

"No one knows for certain," Dafydd answered. "Her grave was not marked, no doubt to prevent any opposing forces that breached the walls from desecrating what would have been an obviously recent burial."

"But why not move her afterward?" It seemed an odd thing for a father to overlook. Dafydd had said Gwen's father yet lived after his daughter's death.

"I do not know," Dafydd said. "That would have been the logical thing to do, but it was never done. This statue was commissioned by her father, and its placement here was overseen by the priest—"

"—Arwyn ap Bedwyr," Griffith tossed in as he continued walking slowly around the angel statue.

Nickolas, himself, had thought about that infamous priest many times in the days since visiting the site of his disreputable burial.

"Neither man, though both had the power and influence to do so, ever had her remains moved to the churchyard."

"Could that be why she is still here, as a ghost, that is?" Griffith asked.

The possibility struck Nickolas. "You mean, perhaps she cannot find peace because she was not properly buried or something of that nature?"

"That I cannot tell you," Dafydd said. "That was not the reason I brought you here to see this."

"Then what?" Could there possibly be more?

Dafydd motioned them both to the other side of the statue, pointing again at the base. A long crack ran perpendicular to the ground and appeared to have been repaired more than once. Centered in the base of the statue was another inscription, again not in English.

"Translation?" he requested.

"You really ought to learn Welsh, Nickolas." Griffith chuckled lightly.

Dafydd was more obliging. "'First of March 1386, to thirty-first of October 1406' is the first line. Those are her birth and death dates. Below that is the inscription, 'Herein lies the means by which our peace was steeply purchased.'"

"These Welshmen had a way with cryptic inscriptions, didn't they?" Nickolas said, recalling the "Be ye chastised and warned" phrase from the priest's grave.

"I cannot say I understand all of what is intended to be said in these inscriptions," Dafydd admitted. "Though I wish I did, for I feel it would tell us more about Gwen."

Nickolas nodded, feeling the same way.

"I showed you this, not because of the inscriptions, though they are intriguing, but in light of the conversation after dinner last night." Dafydd motioned toward the first line etched in the base of the statue, the dates. "Gwen dislikes *Nos Galan Gaeaf* most severely."

Dafydd's tone clearly indicated the statement was significant, but Nickolas didn't know why.

"*October 31*, Nickolas." Griffith had apparently made the connection. "Gwen died on *Nos Galan Gaeaf*."

"Good heavens," Nickolas muttered.

"The date haunts her," Dafydd said. "That sounded like a horrible pun, didn't it?" He shook his head at his own unintentional wording. "It haunts her because, I believe, hers was not a peaceful passing. Whether she was ill or some awful accident befell her, I do not know. She does not talk about her death. But it is a difficult day for her. To have a celebration planned for that very night, I am certain, is hard for her to accept."

Nickolas thought of her reticence the night before. Other than her initial objection to what she had foreseen as a night of inconsiderate taunting, Gwen had not participated in the planning. She had not spoken a word. She had avoided the group.

"So what do we do?" Nickolas asked. "Call off the celebration?"

Dafydd shook his head. "Gwen would never ask that of you."

"Then what?" Nickolas circled the statue again to find himself looking into that grief-stricken face.

"That is something I suggest you ask Gwen."

Chapter Seventeen

One more week. Gwen stared out the window of her room, feeling the pull of The Tower more strongly each hour. Seven more days and she would have to go up there again. Every year as the day drew closer, she grew colder, more weary, more desperate to escape the fate that had been forced on her. This year, she now knew, would be worse than any that had come before it.

She would be up there on *Nos Galan Gaeaf*, as she was required to be, listening to the sounds of a celebration. It would be precisely as it had been three hundred ninety-nine years earlier. She would be suffering while the whole world, it seemed, rejoiced.

"Why is it that I always seem to find you staring out windows?" Nickolas asked from directly beside her. She'd not heard him approach, yet there he stood, leaning with one arm against the window frame. He looked out the window just as she did.

Gwen turned her head to look up at him. As usual, a hint of a smile hovered at the corners of his mouth and an aura of quiet confidence filled his stance. If she had been more than a wisp of a ghost, Gwen would have thrown herself into his arms. She needed the strength she sensed in him, needed the reassurance of his presence and his touch. But such things were little more than wishes for one such as she.

"That was a rather shaky sigh," Nickolas said.

Gwen didn't realize she'd made the rather desperate sound out loud. He gave her a look of such tender understanding, Gwen very nearly sighed again.

"Anything I can do?" he asked.

Her first impulse was to shake her head, but she immediately thought better of it. "Tell me a story," she quietly requested.

"A story?" He sounded thoroughly surprised, which, she acknowledged, he probably was.

"Something lighthearted, happy. Something that will make me smile."

"Are you sad, Gwen?" Nickolas's hand moved momentarily toward her face as if to reassuringly stroke her cheek, but then it dropped back to his side. No doubt he'd remembered he could not possibly touch her.

"A little sad," she confessed.

"Ah." He nodded. Gwen felt certain Nickolas had seen through her insistence that the *Nos Galan Gaeaf* festivities would not disturb her in the least but had been too much of a gentleman to argue with her over it. Neither did he do so again. "Perhaps you would be interested to know that I once fancied myself something of an expert in the area of Arthurian heroics."

He'd adopted that tone she'd grown to love so very much: teasing and encouraging, as well as decidedly empathetic. Gwen was already smiling, her face turned up toward his.

"When I was seven, I staged a rather daring attempt at slaughtering what I was certain was a dragon that had begun wreaking havoc on the area around my cousins' house—I was living with them that summer. The dragon sadly proved to be nothing more than a very badly behaved feral cat."

"Oh, dear." Gwen lightly laughed. "Cats can be vicious."

"As I learned to my detriment." Nickolas held up his left hand. Four very fine, barely visible scars ran across the back of his hand, at least two inches in length. "I tendered my resignation at my own imaginary round table that very afternoon. I did not feel I could be much of a brave knight if I had been bested by a tiny cat."

Gwen could picture the fair-haired little boy Nickolas must once have been dragging a wooden sword dejectedly away from the scene of his humiliation, feeling entirely defeated. She knew the weight of failure well. So often she'd walked away from her own humiliation, head hung, shoulders slumped, hearing her father's frustration with her echoing in her mind with every step.

"I am certain you were all that was brave and heroic." Gwen smiled understandingly.

"I absolutely was." He still leaned with one elbow against the wall, watching her with what looked like fondness. If her heart yet beat in her chest it no doubt would have sped up at that look. "Now it's your turn."

"My turn?" How was it that he managed to make her smile so regularly?

"To tell me a story," he said. "Surely you had some misadventure or another in your childhood. Don't tell me you were a perfect little girl."

A lock of hair had fallen across his forehead. How she would have liked to brush it back, to feel its smoothness between her fingers.

She pulled her gaze away from his hair and focused on his question. "I was far from perfect, I assure you."

"I am anxiously waiting for your story."

He was teasing her again. How she had needed him the past four hundred years.

His childhood recollections had brought one of her own to mind. "I decided when I was eight years old that I was going to train to become a warrior."

"So you fancied yourself a warrior, and I imagined myself a knight." He chuckled. "It seems we were rather destined to meet someday."

"I think maybe we were."

Her sudden serious tone seemed to strike him. Nickolas's gaze softened, his eyes dropping momentarily to her lips. For just a moment, she wondered what it would be like to be kissed by Nickolas Pritchard. The futility of that idea settled on her like a weight.

"How did your warrior adventure play out?" he asked.

For a moment, she did not understand Nickolas's question, so thrown off was she by that fleeting glance at an impossible romance. "Not very well, I'm afraid," she finally managed to say. "I accidentally broke a window, and my father was furious. I had only tried learning to be a warrior to please him, he being quite disappointed at not having a son to whom he could pass down his knowledge. I gave it up after that."

Nickolas did not laugh or make light of her story. "Though no one could question your fire, dearest Gwen"—the endearment brought a smile back to her face—"I cannot at all picture you as a bloodthirsty warrior. You're too sweet."

"I am so grateful you came to Tŷ Mynydd, Nickolas." She would have laid her head on his shoulder if she'd had that ability. "I have been so very lonely here without you."

"Can I tell you something I have never told another soul?"

"Of course. You can tell me anything." She meant it. Never before had she felt such a close connection to anyone. She would trust him with her secrets, just as she hoped he would trust her with his.

"I have been lonely all my life," Nickolas said. "At times, I have been so alone it has hurt."

"Have you felt better since coming here?" She waited anxiously for his reply.

"Infinitely better." He smiled at her, and she knew in that moment that she'd entirely lost her heart to him.

She laid her hand on top of his, only to have it pass through. A feeling swelled up in her, and if she were still living, it would have been accompanied by a sudden and heartrending bout of tears. She turned away, so entirely frustrated.

"Gwen."

"I'm sorry," Gwen whispered, certain he had not appreciated the odd sensation of a ghostly hand passing through his.

"Probably almost as sorry as I am," Nickolas replied, pulling Gwen's gaze back to his face. "I would very much like to have held your hand. I've wanted to before. But . . ."

". . . but I am a ghost," Gwen finished for him.

He didn't answer immediately. The look on his face spoke frustration as poignant and real as her own. "And for that," he said, "I am more sorry than I could possibly express."

Gwen sensed more in his words than sadness at not being able to hold her hand. Hundreds of images flashed through her memory. Remembrances of the countless couples who had called her home their own, of weddings she'd attended, families she'd watched grow in number and in affection. The love she'd seen between so many of those she'd watched be born, grow old, and die would be forever lost to her. And it was a hole in her heart that until that moment, seeing something of those feelings reflected in Nickolas's eyes, she had not felt so painfully and acutely as she ought to have.

"No one has ever said they were sorry I was dead," Gwen whispered, feeling suddenly more weary than she had in hundreds of years.

"Not even your father?" he asked in obvious disbelief. Something in her look must have put the lie to that thought. "He seems to have been a rather unnatural sort of father, then, to have not lamented the loss of a beloved child."

"He did not love me. I realized that some time ago. But in the end, he at least felt that I was useful." She laughed humorlessly. "Every warrior needs a banner to fly, after all. That was my purpose, whether I wished for it or not."

"An *unwilling war cry*," Nickolas said, watching her closely.

She immediately recognized the phrase. "You've seen the angel statue."

"You do not seem to approve of your own monument."

"How could I approve?" Gwen all but snapped. "That insulting attempt by the men who destroyed me to beg for redemption? Did they think merely erecting a monument with a long-suffering angel depicted atop it would serve as restitution for doing what they did?"

Nickolas looked astonished. And well he might be. Gwen had never spoken thus to another person, had never voiced her frustration and anger. Of all the people she'd known, he least deserved her anger.

"I am sorry for yelling, Nickolas. You certainly did not deserve it." She sighed, weary and weighed down. "What they did was wrong. No amount of statuary is going to change that. And all the monuments in the world will not allow me to escape paying the recurrent price of their perfidy."

"Tell me," Nickolas said. "Please. What did they do?"

She could tell he asked not out of morbid curiosity but out of genuine concern. "They saved Y Castell," was all she could bring herself to say. "And the price paid for that guarantee was steep, indeed."

* * *

Nickolas went looking for Gwen the next day. She'd been playing least in sight, forcing him to search for some time. He found her late in the afternoon walking along the long-gone walls of the ancient castle. A cold wind whipped the grounds of Tŷ Mynydd, but as he approached her, Nickolas hardly felt it. How was it that the very sight of Gwen warmed his heart?

"You are a remarkably difficult lady to locate," he called out.

She turned to look at him. Their eyes met, and a smile spread slowly across her beautiful face. Nickolas watched her appreciatively as she floated down to ground level, stopping directly in front of him.

"Good afternoon, Nickolas."

The slight hesitancy that had touched her words seemed to confirm his suspicions. "Have you been avoiding me?"

"Not necessarily. I've simply been . . . not always visible."

"Why have you been hiding from me, Gwen?"

She looked decidedly uncomfortable. How tempted he was to pull her into a reassuring embrace, and how frustrating the realization that he never could.

"I thought you would rather not see me," she said, "after I snapped at you yesterday. That was unfair of me."

"Well, then, let me assure you I not only wished to see you, I have been searching the grounds and house for some time now, trying to find you."

"You have?" A smile suddenly appeared on her face.

"I have." He motioned for her to walk with him, which she did, though 'twas more of a hover. "I had a brilliant idea I wished to run past you."

"Are you looking for my opinion or my approval?"

"Both."

She looked intrigued. Nickolas bit back a smile. He thoroughly enjoyed talking with her. She always held up her end of any conversation and never failed to follow right along with his teasing. Too many young ladies needed prodding or explanations.

"What is this brilliant idea of yours?"

"I want to commission a painting."

Confusion showed in the creasing of her brow. "You seek my approval for a painting?"

Nickolas nodded, entirely serious. "Though you have graciously accepted my ownership, the house really is yours, and I want your opinion and, yes, your approval."

She gave every indication of being flattered. "I have said it before but will do so again: you are a good man, Nickolas Pritchard."

"Let me tell you about this painting, and then you can decide if I am a good man or a foolish one."

"What in heaven's name have you decided to have painted?" An amused laugh mingled with her tone of curiosity.

Nickolas could have happily spent every day of his life walking with her just like he was then. The grounds sat peacefully inviting all around them. The cares and concerns of the day faded into the background.

"I wish to have a painting done of the old castle," he said.

"But Y Castell no longer stands, Nickolas. How could any artist accurately paint something that no longer exists?"

A gust tugged at his coat but had no noticeable impact on her. He hoped that meant she did not feel the biting wind. She was not dressed at all warmly enough for the recent drop in temperature. He would have offered her his coat if the gesture would have done any good.

"I have found a few sketches of it in the library," Nickolas said, "though none of them are complete, all apparently having been rendered after it began to crumble."

"You wish for a painting of it as it stood when whole?" She gave him a wary look, and he wondered at it.

"Not if it will upset you," he quickly replied. "That was not my intention at all."

"I never thought it was," she said. "Of all the people who have ever resided here, you have never once seemed determined to upset me or overlook my feelings or desires."

Her assessment touched him. "Your feelings are of paramount importance to me, Gwen. I actually first conceived of the idea of having the castle painted because of you."

She once more appeared pleasantly curious. His simple words of reassurance had succeeded in wiping the wariness from her face.

"I thought you might appreciate being able to see it again," he said. "You must miss it sometimes."

She nodded. "I do have some very happy memories of the old castle."

"Perhaps you would be willing to fill in the missing details so the rendering can be complete and true to the original."

She did not answer immediately. Nickolas watched her as they continued their slow amble across the grounds. Her expression was decidedly contemplative. He hoped her recollections were pleasant ones. He knew all too well that she had many unhappy memories—he'd seen evidence of that fact on her face many times.

"Could it be painted as it looked in the spring?" she asked. "It was always so beautiful in the spring."

He stepped in front of her, grateful when she stopped before passing through him. "This painting, Gwen, is for you. The castle will be painted however you wish to remember it."

"I get to choose the memories I keep?"

He hadn't considered it in quite that way. "I suppose that's the idea," he said.

She closed her eyes. He'd never seen anyone stand so perfectly still. "I would wish to remember the castle as it was while my mother was alive." Unmistakable longing filled her words.

"Then do remember it that way."

Gwen looked at him once more, resignation and sadness in her eyes. "It's not that simple, Nickolas. Some things aren't easy to forget."

What things? he wondered. Asking her outright would be unforgivably presumptuous. "What can I do?" he asked instead.

She smiled a little. "Have I told you how much I appreciate that you treat me as though I actually matter?"

"You *do* actually matter."

Her smile grew a bit. "How fearsome you look just now."

"Fearsome?" He stepped closer, raising an eyebrow.

"Yes, fearsome." A mischievous expression lit her face. "And I confess I enjoy it immensely. No one has ever stood up for me before."

"Which brings me back to my original question. What can I do about these memories you can't manage to forget?"

"Tell me a story."

He studied her a moment, wanting to see if she was indeed serious. Sincerity radiated from her. "Another story?"

"Yes, please. I enjoyed the last one."

They took up their walk once more, while Nickolas searched his mind for something that might amuse her. He knew she asked him in order to distract her, not because a tale would actually solve any of her problems. Still, a lighthearted story wasn't much to ask. He would do anything for her, anything at all.

"I lived with a cousin of my mother when I was eleven."

"The same cousin as when you were seven?" she asked.

He shook his head. "I was passed from relative to relative. I'd live with one for a few months, sometimes as long as a year, and they'd tire of me and send me to someone else."

"Which must be the reason for the loneliness you spoke of before."

It was, indeed. "After my parents died, I never truly had a family again. I wanted one more than anything else in my whole life."

"It is a hard thing to be alone in this world."

Others had expressed similar sentiments. From Gwen, however, it held greater significance. "You and I have known a great deal of loneliness, haven't we?"

She nodded and sighed. "Far too much." Some of her sadness lifted. "But less now. I am not so lonely with you here."

"The feeling is mutual." Nickolas reached for her hand, but his fingers met only empty air. He clasped his hands behind his back, knowing the temptation to touch her would not dissipate, despite the illogical nature of that inclination. The more time he spent in her company, the more he longed for her.

"When you were eleven . . ." Gwen prodded, reminding Nickolas that he had been telling a story.

"When I was eleven"—he gave her a grin—"I decided I would make my fortune as an inventor."

Gwen appeared appropriately amused. "What did you invent?"

"I *attempted* to invent a great many things. My first failure involved a combined knife and fork, which, it turns out, is impossible to actually use."

Her little giggle made his heart jump in his chest.

"I next tried my hand at designing a clothes horn."

"What is a clothes horn?"

Nickolas could not have asked for a more gratifyingly curious response. "I imagined a stick of some kind that a gentleman could use to get his own jacket on, no matter how ridiculously tight fashions became."

"And did every valet in the county rise up in fear for their positions?"

He shook his head. "Trust me, they had nothing to worry about. I could not manage to perfect the idea."

"How many other ideas did you work on?"

"Scores."

Gwen grinned at him. "And never made your fortune."

Nickolas chuckled. "Obviously not."

"I should have liked to have known you as a boy."

He clasped his hands more tightly behind his back, the urge to wrap his arm around her misty shoulders almost overwhelming. "But I have told you only the amusing moments of my younger years. You likely would have found my troublemaking and moments of self-pity quite trying."

"I would have loved every part of you," she whispered.

That declaration left him utterly speechless. How perfectly she'd expressed the very feelings surging through his heart. He couldn't imagine not loving everything about her.

He opened his mouth to tell her as much but found the words caught. What could be gained by confessing how deeply he'd come to love her? Nothing could come of his feelings. There could be no future. He would only burden her by admitting the state of his heart when the situation was, when it came down to it, utterly hopeless.

Chapter Eighteen

"The masquerade should be quite lovely," Miss Castleton said to Nickolas as they walked through the gardens behind the house.

Mr. and Mrs. Castleton had insisted on the excursion. They had, in fact, arranged several such private moments between the two over the course of the house party, ranging from morning rides to leisurely walks to afternoon picnics. More than once, Dafydd had been obliged to give up his conversational partner so that Nickolas could indulge the Castletons.

"I think it will be," Nickolas answered. "There will be quite a large number of guests, though not so many as to make the hall too crowded."

Miss Castleton smiled in her sweet way, and Nickolas found himself smiling in return. He had a certain fondness for her, though he could not, in any honesty, describe his feelings as surpassing, rivaling, or even coming close to those he felt for Gwen. But Gwen, as he had to continually remind himself, was an unobtainable wish. She was dead, a ghost wandering the corridors of his home. There was no future between a man yet living and a lady dead for nearly four hundred years. It was a frustrating and impossible situation, but one he would have to learn to live with. Nothing else could be done.

"This is a beautiful area of the country." Miss Castleton looked around her in obvious admiration of the countryside. "Mr. Evans says that the Tŷ Mynydd valley is a very good representation of the beauties of Wales."

"I understand that is true," Nickolas said. "It would be enjoyable, I think, to see more of Wales."

"I agree." She smiled in a friendly manner. "My parents hope to return here again and again over the years."

"Do they?" Nickolas forced a swallow.

Mr. Castleton had hinted at those very intentions only the day before. He had more than hinted at a great many other things, including the expectations Nickolas's invitation had given rise to in all of their hearts and minds. He had not, he knew, kept his interest in Miss Castleton a secret before his inheritance, and his pointed attentions since would simply have reaffirmed his intentions.

He might, if he tried, be able to extricate himself from making the offer that was obviously expected of him. It would not precisely be gentlemanly of him, but if he'd had any hope of making a future with the woman he loved, he would have managed it.

What would be the point, he'd asked himself repeatedly the night before. He'd be going through life essentially as a widower, a man who'd lost the woman he loved. Except that he'd never actually had her—she'd died long before he was born. He'd find growing frustration in her companionship and, he knew, would regret the loss of children and a family.

What hope did he have? Gwen was lost to him. He did not wish to live out his life alone.

The Castletons expected an offer to be forthcoming. A gentleman did not knowingly, and he had to admit he'd known he was doing so, raise expectations in a gently bred young lady without fulfilling those expectations. And when said gentleman had no hope of a life with the woman he loved, making a life with a woman he at least liked and who seemed to like him in return was about as promising a future as he could hope for.

"Are you fond of me, Miss Castleton?" The question did not seem to catch her off guard.

"Of course I am, Mr. Pritchard."

"And you do realize why your parents have been throwing us together so determinedly, do you not?"

She smiled a little shyly and nodded.

"And you do not object to their reasons?"

"I do not, Mr. Pritchard." Why did that answer feel like a lead weight instead of the reassurance it ought to have been?

A man ought not to make a proposal in a spirit of resignation. There seemed little choice and even less hope.

"Would you do me the honor, then, Miss Castleton, of becoming my wife?"

She nodded once more and smiled a little.

As simply as that, their futures were decided. Nickolas couldn't help but notice that neither of them appeared overly happy about it.

* * *

For once, Mr. Castleton held every eye in the room for a reason other than that he was making a spectacle of himself. He stood in the midst of the assembled guests in the drawing room after dinner and made it known that he had an announcement to make.

The butler had been forewarned and stood, Nickolas knew, just outside the door with champagne at the ready. Mr. Castleton looked ready to burst and, for the first time, seemed to have forgotten all about Gwen. Mrs. Castleton was already dabbing at her eyes. Miss Castleton, Nickolas noted with some dissatisfaction, looked rather more pale than usual.

Mr. Castleton finally spoke. "It is my pleasure to announce that my daughter, Charlotte, has received an offer of marriage from our host, Mr. Nickolas Pritchard, and that she has accepted him."

Exclamations of happiness, if not surprise, could be heard around the room as the butler entered with champagne ready to be distributed. Miss Castleton received hugs from the female guests. Nickolas received a few hearty slaps on the back.

"Are you sure about this?" Griffith asked in low tones.

Nickolas nodded, though he couldn't be certain the gesture was convincing.

Griffith hesitated a moment, studying him. "Then I am happy for you." He smiled his congratulations.

One expression of happiness was notably absent, and Nickolas found himself unable to account for it.

Still seated and seemingly in a state of shock, Dafydd looked almost ashen. The smile that always seemed to lurk just under the surface was entirely missing. Even as Nickolas watched, the ever-amiable vicar seemed to pull himself together once more. He rose slowly and crossed to Nickolas.

"Congratulations," he said, his tone a bit halfhearted. "Miss Castleton is a fine lady."

"She is."

Dafydd offered nothing more than that. He bowed quite correctly to Miss Castleton but said nothing. She avoided his gaze, much as she had the first time they'd met, though Nickolas realized she hadn't done so in the weeks that had followed. In fact, they had seemed on friendly terms, often seen sitting near one another or engaged in light conversation.

Nickolas did not attend very closely to the toasts being made in his and his affianced bride's honor. His eyes followed Dafydd, who was making a somewhat hasty retreat. A moment before Nickolas's friend reached the door, Gwen came through it. Nickolas could barely make out their words over the voices around him.

"A celebration?" Gwen asked, looking confused.

"Yes," Dafydd said, rather tightly. "Nickolas and Miss Castleton are recently engaged."

Gwen's eyes swung to Nickolas, locking with them. Dafydd slipped around her and out the door, but Gwen remained. Her eyes shifted only once to glance briefly at Miss Castleton.

"You are engaged?" She spoke in a voice so soft that her words hardly carried.

He couldn't manage any words but merely nodded.

Gwen looked at him a moment longer before leaving. She did not slip through a wall, nor kick up a whirlwind.

She simply hung her head in a posture of complete, dejected defeat and vanished.

*　*　*

It was the closest Gwen had come in four hundred years to experiencing physical pain. Feelings, she had learned during her never-ending tenure at Tŷ Mynydd, could be as unendurable as the deepest wound. The emotional blow she had only just received would likely pain her long after a physical wound would have healed.

She sat hovering near the floor in a corner of her room, wishing she had the ability to simply cry. A bout of tears might not erase the pain and misery she was enduring, but it would have been a welcome release.

How could she bear it? She would be forced to watch Nickolas marry, raise his family, love his wife. She, who loved him so very much, would have to endure it all in silence, unable to look forward to any sort of future, unable to escape. His great-grandchildren would walk the corridors of Tŷ Mynydd, and she would be there still, loving him, alone, seeing him in his offspring, thinking of those fleeting weeks once upon a time when he had made her smile, when he had unknowingly laid claim to her heart. She would die a hundred times over and never find a moment's peace.

A knock broke the silence of the room.

Gwen sighed in mingled frustration and devastation. It was no doubt Mr. Castleton, come to stare at her for hours on end and ask impertinent questions. She kept silent in the hope that he would simply go away and leave her to her own suffering. A moment later, however, she heard a key turn in the lock.

How had the man gotten hold of a key to her room?

Gwen slid into invisibility and kept to her shadowed corner. He would eventually give up. Perhaps by morning, he would have left and she could return to her peaceful solitude.

But it was not the gaping Mr. Castleton who entered her room. It was Nickolas.

"Gwen?" he asked, looking around at the seemingly empty room. He called out to her once more after closing and locking the door behind him. Still, she did not answer. She could not bear the thought of speaking to him, of attempting to act as though her pathetic excuse for an existence had not entirely crumbled when Dafydd told her of Nickolas's engagement.

He stopped not far from the window, looking around him, his expression one of concern. "I know you are in here." His voice barely rose above a whisper. "I cannot even say how I know, only that I do." He paused, obviously waiting for her to confirm his words, casting his eyes about the room. She neither moved nor spoke. Somehow, it was easier that way. "Please don't hide from me, Gwen."

His pleading tone nearly undid her. But she found a certain heart-breaking solace in her invisibility. Given time, he would forget about her, forget that she wandered the corridors of the home he shared with his wife and family. All of Tŷ Mynydd would forget. She would simply walk the long-since fallen walls of her one-time home unseen and unheeded and find a quiet corner to spend her days and nights. Time would continue its relentless march until that day's suffering was little but a memory, held only by herself.

"I am sorry you found out the way you did," Nickolas said. She knew without further clues that he referred to his own engagement. "I had intended to tell you myself, but . . ." He stopped and took a shaky breath. Nickolas pushed his fingers through his hair. "Sometimes life is terribly unfair, Gwen. If only one of us had been born at a different time, four hundred years earlier or later than we were."

If she hadn't been a ghost, Gwen would have wept. *Unfair* did not even begin to describe how fate had treated her.

"I have never had a family." Nickolas sat on the edge of her bed just as he had several times before whilst they'd spoken with so much natural ease and friendliness. "I have always wanted one. I have always wanted, if I ever was fortunate enough to have the means to support a family, to have children and a wife and a home. And . . ." Again, he pushed out a difficult breath. "That kind of future, *any* kind of future, is impossible with a lady who is already dead."

Despite her determination to remain undetected, the slightest of breezes picked up in the room at the pain his well-intentioned words inflicted.

Nickolas watched the fluttering window curtains with a look of resignation that must have matched her own. "Miss Castleton is a fine lady, kindhearted and good-natured. I believe she will make a good wife." His gaze broke away from the swaying curtains and moved quickly around the room. Gwen knew he was looking for her. "I have to try to make some sort of a life for myself, Gwen." A hint of determination entered his tone. He rose to his feet. "I just wanted you to know why. And that . . . that I do care about you. I just can't . . . I am making the best of a difficult situation and have every intention of being happy. I hope that you can as well. I want you to be."

Happy? Gwen knew she would not be. In time, she might find some degree of contentment. In the meantime, she would keep her suffering and herself concealed and allow the world around her to move ahead and leave her behind.

Nickolas stood up and walked silently to the door. Over his shoulder he offered a heavy "Good night, Gwen" and was gone, the door locked once more behind him.

It was the way things had to be. He would create a life for himself, and she would fade into memory. In her invisibility, she would find a semblance of escape from the pain of losing him whom she had never truly had to begin with. They had had their last conversation, their last moment of friendly interaction. She had known the joy of his eyes locked with her own for the final time.

"Good-bye, Nickolas," Gwen whispered into the empty room.

Chapter Nineteen

GWEN HADN'T ANTICIPATED LOSING HER sanctuary. The room remained locked, except for the daily dusting the maids continued to undertake. 'Twas not an invasion that drove her from her room but her own memories. The peace and solace she'd once known there had vanished. The chamber reminded her of Nickolas and how much she missed him already, despite only three days having passed without his company.

She avoided the house entirely now. At night she walked the fallen walls of Y Castell, silent and lost. During the daylight hours, when the house teemed with activity, its occupants appearing without warning, she traversed the farthest corners of the estate where no one ever ventured.

But loneliness overtook her on the third day of her exile, driving her to the one person other than Nickolas she would have most liked to have near at hand to soothe her aching heart. She stood at her mother's headstone on the side opposite her father's grave. That the two were buried beside one another had kept her away more often than not over the centuries.

Gwen's own monument stood several rows behind her. She kept her back determinedly toward it.

Nickolas had promised her she could remember the castle in any way she chose. Often over the previous three days, she had closed her eyes and pictured it as whole and strong as it had been in her childhood, the angel statue gone, her mother yet living, and Nickolas himself come as a suitor seeking her hand. She imagined him taking her away from Y Castell before the arrival of King Henry's troops, before warfare and cruelty robbed her of everything. Inevitably, however, the daydreams dissolved, and reality returned in all its ugliness.

"Oh, Mama," she said. "Why must fate continually crush me?"

She glanced over at her father's grave. He who actually deserved the punishment she endured had escaped it all after only a handful of years.

She'd once longed for his affection and approval but had found, after the passage of so many painful years, that she could not think of her father without hating him. Gwen decided long ago not to let his memory poison her, so she thought of him as seldom as possible.

Pushing her father firmly from her mind, Gwen once more addressed her absent mother, wishing she could truly talk to her again. "I am so very lonely, Mother. I have no one to talk to, no one to care about me. Another four hundred years of this will drive me mad, and yet there is no escape. Perhaps I could come talk with you on occasion, when I am particularly lonesome. As I sincerely doubt you and Father are in the same location"—heaven hardly seemed the appropriate final destination for him—"I need not worry about him overhearing. This is all his fault, you know. All of it."

There was no answer beyond complete silence. These would be one-sided conversations, a dissatisfying stand-in for the company of another person.

She allowed her eyes to wander to the distant house, where Nickolas was likely just having his breakfast. Only a week earlier, she would have turned to him for a jovial story to liven her spirits. They would have wandered the grounds or the house and simply talked.

"I cannot recall the last time I saw you in the churchyard, Gwen."

She spun at the sound of Dafydd's voice. Her distraction had allowed him to approach unnoticed, without a thought given to whether or not she'd remained invisible.

"Good morning, Dafydd. I had not meant to disturb you. I came to"—she found herself reluctant to admit the purpose of her visit but did so anyway—"visit my mother."

He did not laugh at the futility of her effort. Something like empathy crossed his face. "No one has seen you these past few days," Dafydd said.

"The household has been occupied with planning the upcoming festivities. I imagine they have been too busy to notice me." She managed the lie with a convincing degree of casualness.

Dafydd nodded. "The engagement has only added to the chaos, I'm afraid."

"Do they seem happy?" Though she strove for a tone of disinterest, Gwen knew she fell quite far from the mark.

Dafydd studied her rather more closely than was comfortable. Understanding dawned in his features. Gwen braced herself, not knowing how he would respond. "You've fallen in love with him, haven't you?"

She wanted to believe it was compassion and not pity that colored his tone. There would be no avoiding the question, and she could not feel comfortable lying to a man of the cloth on the grounds of a church. "Quite hopelessly, I'm afraid."

"Hopeless." He repeated that single word with a nod of understanding.

Hearing him confirm her evaluation of the situation only broke her heart further.

"Will you come to the wedding?" he asked. "You have never missed one in four hundred years."

She had pondered that very question again and again since learning of Nickolas's engagement. "The neighborhood will surely notice if I do not make an appearance."

"That they will," Dafydd agreed. "And will likely see it as evidence that you disapprove of Tŷ Mynydd's newest master and his bride."

Gwen sighed. "I cannot do that to either of them."

"Then you will subject yourself to the sight of watching the one you love marry another?" An odd mixture of empathy and surprise colored his words.

"Perhaps you ought to warn the ladies to secure their bonnets—the chapel is likely to be a bit windy." She tried for a joking tone but failed quite miserably.

Neither of them spoke as they stood on that bit of hallowed ground. She knew not what occupied Dafydd's thoughts. Hers were quite firmly on Nickolas, as they had been so often since his arrival at Tŷ Mynydd. How she loved him! And she would be forced to watch him marry. She would endure that to ensure his acceptance in the neighborhood, to make his life a little easier.

"Might I ask you a question, Dafydd, as a man of the cloth?"

His attention returned to her. "Are you in need of spiritual advisement?"

She nodded.

"You may ask anything you wish."

"I have thought back on the twenty years of my life, and I cannot think of anything I might have done to warrant four hundred years of penance. Dying young seems harsh enough but would not have been so terrible if I'd been permitted to actually move on. I might have been with my mother all these years." The wind kicked up by her sadness mingled with the late October breeze. "Why must life be so very unfair?"

"I don't think any of us understands why good people must pass through so much pain." Dafydd's expression seemed to indicate he too had experienced undeserved difficulties. "We simply must learn from them and live the best life we can until our sojourn is over."

She held her hands out in frustration. "But my sojourn will never be over. My lot is centuries of loss piled atop pain piled atop suffering. There is no end to it."

Dafydd looked apologetic but offered no words of solace. He likely had none to give.

"Do you know why I avoid the cemetery?" she asked.

"The angel?"

"That statue is certainly a factor," Gwen acknowledged. "But it is more than that. I look around at all these names, and I envy them. They have found rest. Most, I am certain, have passed on to their reward. Their struggles here are over, and I envy them that. It is not a peaceful feeling to endure."

"You wish to move on?"

Sorrow cut deeply into her. "More now than ever before."

"He has truly broken your heart, hasn't he?"

She allowed herself to begin fading into invisibility. "Life has broken my heart. Irrevocably."

"Can I do anything for you?"

"Pray for me, Dafydd. Pray for a merciful release from this never-ending anguish."

A harsh wind whipped at the grounds around them.

"And is there anything you'd like me to tell Nickolas?"

She shook her head. "I think it best to allow him to forget I ever existed." Invisibility cloaked her entirely as she spoke those final words.

"I will pray for you, Gwen," Dafydd said, his eyes searching around.

She did not respond out loud but thought, *Perhaps God will listen to* you.

* * *

Life at Tŷ Mynydd little resembled what it had been a mere few days earlier. Miss Castleton had grown discouragingly quiet even as her mother had grown far more vociferous. There was talk of a Christmas wedding at the Tŷ Mynydd chapel, though Dafydd, who had lost a great deal of his usual outgoing, friendly nature, was being very elusive as to his availability to perform the ceremony. Griffith had taken to silent studies of Nickolas and Miss Castleton, though he never revealed what he was searching for. Mr. Castleton was in a pother over the glaring absence of Gwen, something that weighed on Nickolas as well.

She had not, since the first day of the house party, been so entirely absent. Her presence had always been felt, either in the form of mysterious winds or by an actual appearance. Even on those days when she did not cross paths with one or more of the houseguests, she had been seen at a distance. But four days had passed without a single soul seeing even a fleeting glimpse of her. The maids who tended her room found it empty. The grooms who had nightly seen her walking the now-fallen walls of the ancient castle reported not so much as a hint of her.

"You don't suppose she has up and left?" Mr. Castleton asked more than once. He'd sounded more annoyed than concerned.

Dafydd had explained to him that Gwen was inextricably tied to Tŷ Mynydd and could not have left. He had hazarded a guess that she simply chose not to be seen. Something in the tone of Dafydd's voice as he had said as much told Nickolas that the usually social vicar wished he had the ability to disappear as well.

Mrs. Davis seemed to have sensed the sudden weight hanging over the guests and had been making valiant attempts to garner enthusiasm for the upcoming *Nos Galan Gaeaf* festivities. She met with only minimal success, despite the combined efforts of her family members.

Nickolas tried his utmost not to think of Gwen, to wonder where she might be, to worry about whether or not she had forgiven him. He had grasped at what little hope he had, while it seemed she was left with none at all. She could not escape, could not make her own future. She was, he was absolutely certain, hiding from them all, enduring the pain he felt but doing so utterly alone. Nickolas missed her most especially in the quiet, lonely hours of the night. He would have to exorcise the thoughts of her that continually invaded his mind. It was not fair to self-inflict such torture, nor would it be fair to Miss Castleton for him to enter into a marriage with a disloyal mind and heart.

Nos Galan Gaeaf dawned at Tŷ Mynydd under this newly oppressive atmosphere. Rather than awaking with his mind full of thoughts of the festivities or that night's masquerade ball, Nickolas couldn't expunge the reminder that this was the day three hundred ninety-nine years earlier that Gwen had died.

He pulled on a heavy overcoat, it having snowed the night before, and made his way to the stables. He decided in the quiet hours of the morning that he would ride to the churchyard and find Gwen's statue so he might say his good-byes. He'd been unable to do so with her in person, and with Gwen's continued self-imposed exile, it seemed unlikely he would.

Dafydd was just leaving the chapel when Nickolas rode up. "All's well?"

Nickolas nodded, though he wondered if it was truly wise to tell such an enormous bouncer in a churchyard. He half expected to be felled by lightning. "I just needed a little peace and quiet." Nickolas added to his sins by throwing out another lie.

Dafydd smiled empathetically. "You would not be the first to come here seeking just that."

"And do these seekers find what they are looking for?"

"That depends on the burdens they are carrying."

Nickolas mulled that over. His burdens arose from frustration and hopelessness. A walk through a cemetery hardly seemed likely to alleviate that.

"Preparations for tonight's ball are underway, then?" Dafydd said, his smile seeming a little forced. It had been that way lately. Dafydd had been playing rather least in sight as well. He hadn't made it to Tŷ Mynydd for dinner the last two nights in a row. It seemed odd that a vicar in such a small community would suddenly be too busy with duties to come for dinner.

Nickolas nodded in response to Dafydd's question.

"The chapel is not locked up," Dafydd offered.

Nickolas shook his head. "I am too restless for indoors." *And telling far too many lies for the inside of a church.*

"The churchyard is always peaceful. Of course, tonight I wouldn't advise being here." He even managed a small smile. "*Nos Galan Gaeaf,* you know. The spirits of the dead walk the earth tonight. Graveyards are generally considered best avoided."

Nickolas smiled back. "I'll take my chances this morning."

Dafydd nodded. "I need to make a walk about the yard myself. The first hard freeze of the year, like we had last night, always seems to topple a grave marker or two. I'd offer to walk along with you, but I could use a little solitude too."

Nickolas didn't pry. Though he felt a bit of concern for his friend, he didn't ask what weighed on Dafydd. He needed the time alone to close a chapter in his life, a chapter that had ended hardly before it had begun.

The angel statue was easy to find but difficult to look upon. The suffering so apparent on the statue cut at Nickolas's very heart. He'd seen that expression of pain in Gwen's eyes in the moments after she learned of his engagement. He saw it in the flash of realization that he'd chosen a path in life that did not, could not truly, include her. Did she realize he hadn't wanted to? Did she know that the choice had ripped him apart? What else could he have done? The life he wanted, the one with her, was nothing but an impossible dream.

He dropped his eyes to the base of the monument, the stone box on which the statue stood.

The inscription, he remembered, spoke of Gwen's protective role at Tŷ Mynydd. And if memory served, it asked for her forgiveness. That was, Nickolas thought ruefully, ironically fitting. He felt the need to beg her forgiveness himself. Yet it was not his fault that they were separated. It was fate—cruel, unfeeling fate.

He looked once more into the face of the stone angel and could almost picture himself looking at her. "I am sorry, Gwen," he whispered. "Sorry I was born four hundred years too late. Sorry I am living while you are dead. I am sorry you are alone."

A few rows away Dafydd was making his inspection of the ancient cemetery, checking the sturdiness of gravestones that had stood for hundreds of years. How many of those people had Gwen watched throughout their lives? How long would she be forced to remain behind while all around her the people she knew passed on? And how was it that heaven or fate, whichever was responsible, could ask such a cruel price of her?

Herein lies the means by which our peace was steeply purchased. The other side of the monument Gwen despised had said that, according to Dafydd.

The price paid for that guarantee was steep, indeed. Those had been Gwen's words. Again, a price, a purchase. *They saved Y Castell.* That was the guarantee. *Peace*, as the monument said.

But what exactly had been the price? Nickolas knew Gwen herself had served as an inspiration to those who'd fought for their home. But what had her father and the priest done that Gwen had condemned? What had they done to "save Y Castell"?

He circled to the back side of the statue, intending to cross the churchyard back to his mount. The trip to Gwen's monument hadn't given him the sense of closure he'd been searching for. But he had the sinking suspicion he would not see Gwen again and, therefore, couldn't satisfactorily conclude this journey.

Another frustrated look at the statue brought Nickolas's attention to the crack he'd noticed the first time he'd come there. "Dafydd," he called out over his shoulder, keeping his eyes on the crack, which had opened up despite the previous mending. "I think I have found a casualty."

"A casualty?" Dafydd asked when he'd reached Nickolas's side.

Nickolas pointed to the crack along the base of the statue.

Dafydd made a noise of acknowledgment. "That crack always reopens this time of year—the freezing temperatures. I'll have to have the mason look at this when he comes by on his repairing rounds. It is not so bad it cannot be saved."

Which was a shame, Nickolas thought. Gwen disliked the statue with a passion. Seeing it come down would not, he thought, be something to mourn.

Just then the midmorning sun glinted off something just within the crack at the base of the statue. Nickolas sat back on his haunches and thrust a gloved finger inside, only to find the crack a hair too narrow. His gloves came off, and he tried again.

"What is it, Nickolas?"

"I'm not sure. I saw something. Just inside."

Dafydd squatted beside him, looking as well. "I see it. Something metal, I'd guess."

Nickolas nodded and made another attempt. A successful one this time. From inside the hollow, broken base of the statue Gwen's father and his cohort, the priest, had erected came a single, heavy, centuries-old key.

Chapter Twenty

"YOUR GUESTS WILL CERTAINLY NOTICE their host is absent," Griffith said, reminding Nickolas again of his duties.

In one hand, Nickolas held his mask, a plain black one that covered his face around his eyes but, in reality, disguised nothing. His other hand still held the key he'd found in the graveyard that morning. "I cannot shake the feeling that this is something significant," he said, studying it for the hundredth time.

"I don't doubt that it is," Dafydd said. "Though I'd rather not wager on it."

Nickolas smiled at the memory of their now infamous bet. "You're suggesting I let this mystery wait until the morning."

"That would be advisable." He straightened the cuffs of his formal jacket—they were moments from going down to the ball. Though Dafydd hadn't cried off, he'd been noticeably lacking in enthusiasm. "Miss Castleton, I am sure, is expecting her fiancé to at least be present at tonight's ball."

There was no arguing with that. As a newly engaged man, and the host of the night's gathering, Nickolas needed to pull himself together and throw himself into his roles. Miss Castleton deserved that consideration at the very least. He suspected she knew he didn't feel a desperate love for her. She didn't seem likely to chastise him for being neglectful, but she deserved his attention. Gwen, on the other hand, would have let him know in excessively forceful terms precisely what he was doing wrong. She would have expected his very best in everything he did. She would make him want to live up to those expectations.

A sad, longing sort of smile spread across Nickolas's face. While he appreciated Miss Castleton's tenderness, he loved Gwen's spark of life. Ironic, considering it was utter lack of *life* that had robbed them of their shared future.

Nickolas shook his head to clear his thoughts. He must learn some discipline where Gwen was concerned. Thinking of her, longing for her, would only bring more heartache. He could be happy with Miss Castleton. He *knew* he could be. They got along well enough, and she was a good-hearted lady. They would not be deliriously happy, nor would theirs be the love story he might have lived, but they could be happy. Dwelling on thoughts of what could not be would not help nor would it be appropriate.

He slipped the mysterious key into an inside pocket of his jacket and tied his black mask into place. It felt fitting to wear a disguise. He had to hide his feelings, his heartbreak—why not hide his very face? Someday, he told himself, it would not be such a struggle.

Dafydd and Griffith walked at Nickolas's side as they made their way from his sitting room down to the entry hall at the front of the house. Miss Castleton stood below, talking quietly with Mrs. Davis. It had been decided that Miss Castleton, as Nickolas's fiancée, would be joining the reception line. She wore a dress of copper that complemented her coloring perfectly, and yet, all Nickolas could muster was a vague feeling of appreciation. He would have to work on recapturing the feelings she had once inspired. Having something now to compare with those feelings, Nickolas realized his impressions of her had rarely strayed beyond appreciation. He realized he'd never truly loved her.

Somewhere just beyond the weight of his own worries, Nickolas took note of a sharp intake of breath from Dafydd as they first turned the corner to the entry hall and Miss Castleton came into view. She had that effect on people, Nickolas acknowledged. Griffith, however, seemed immune.

When Nickolas glanced at his friend, Dafydd was not looking at Miss Castleton. In fact, he seemed to be pointedly *not* looking at Miss Castleton. Who was in turn decidedly looking away from Dafydd.

"Have you and Miss Castleton exchanged harsh words?" Nickolas asked under his breath. It would be just one more difficulty heaped on top of the rest if one of his two best friends and his soon-to-be bride didn't get along.

"No," Dafydd reassured him, an uncharacteristic sadness in his tone. "No harsh words. I assure you I hold your future bride in highest esteem."

"Then why do you sound so blasted depressed?"

Dafydd smiled but not happily. What was bothering the man?

Griffith made a pondering noise, now directing the look of examination he'd been using on Nickolas for days at Dafydd.

The arrival of guests pushed all other thoughts to the back of Nickolas's mind. He had at least met all of the guests before, though some were still very unfamiliar. They were locals and knew that Tŷ Mynydd was supposed to be haunted. They looked alternately intrigued and concerned. Nickolas reassured them and insisted there were no dangerous specters in residence. Indeed, he would have been hard-pressed to prove there were any specters at all. Gwen had not been seen in a week's time.

Nickolas and Miss Castleton opened the ball with an almost stiff, extremely awkward minuet. A palpable feeling of relief emerged between them when other couples joined the dance. Nickolas attempted to strike up a friendly conversation, but Miss Castleton seemed . . . sad. 'Twas not an auspicious beginning.

* * *

Time was growing short. Gwen could feel the vaguely familiar sensation closing in around her. Another few minutes and she would be forced to go through it all again. Three hundred ninety-eight times she'd endured the fear, the pain, the terror of that night. Her only consolation lay in knowing that while she relived it, she would remember nothing that had happened since that original night. She would be able to hold to the ignorant assumption that somehow she would escape.

Two stories below her room, the ball was well underway. She'd watched the carriages pull up, seen the guests arrive. Nickolas was down there with all of them, dancing with his future bride. What Gwen wouldn't have given in that moment to have had him there beside her.

"Please save me from this." Gwen spoke into the emptiness, her heart breaking with her loneliness and helplessness. The only answering sound was that of music floating up through the chill October night.

She would be alone in her suffering, as always.

Slowly, an unearthly fog began to creep into the room. Ghostly remnants of her room as it had once stood materialized around her. Whispers of the heavy furniture of centuries gone by took form in the room. Behind the sheer white curtains she loved so much hung a phantom set of tapestries, the very same that had hung there on the last night of her life. The night's transformation had begun. She would forget everything soon. She would not recall four hundred years of quiet and attempts at healing. She would not remember the fortified castle slowly giving way to the peaceful house that now stood. She would not remember the victories the next hours had ensured.

She would not remember *him.*

"Oh, Nickolas," Gwen whispered in anguish. "Please help me. Do not leave me to face this alone."

The fog grew thick and heavy around her. From across the chasm of centuries, her father called out to her.

"Gwenllian," his booming voice echoed in the vast emptiness. In his precise and rumbling Welsh, he added the words her tender heart, desperate for his love and affection, could not resist: "Come, dear girl. Your *dadi* is in desperate need of your company."

"I am coming directly, Father," she answered, smiling at his kind words. If only he could be thus always!

In the back of her mind a memory nagged: a pair of merry blue eyes and fair hair. A name hovered unidentifiably on her lips, only to fade into nothingness. And why she longed for him, she couldn't remember.

Her father called to her again, and she hastened to obey.

* * *

A collective gasp sounded around the ballroom. Nickolas knew without even looking that Gwen had made an appearance at last. He told his heart to settle even as it began to beat ever harder. He hadn't seen her in a week, a week that felt like a lifetime. But would seeing her again be soothing or torturous?

Several of the guests moved anxiously to one side or the other, opening up Nickolas's view of Gwen moving gracefully across the ballroom. She appeared to be walking quickly, lightly, though her steps made no sound.

Gwen's face turned so she looked directly at Nickolas but did not, somehow, appear to see him. She was smiling, a different sort of smile than he had ever seen her wear. The weight of sadness that she forever carried with her had vanished. She appeared lighthearted, free, unburdened. There was such innocent joy on her face.

Nickolas stood stunned, speechless. A need, almost desperate, rose up in him to see that look on her face always. That look of hopeful happiness belonged to her. It was, he knew without being told, an expression that once came naturally to her.

He opened his mouth to say something, anything, that might halt her long enough for him to memorize her countenance. She seemed oblivious to the stares of the pressing crowd. Gwen continued her joyous half run.

An instant too late, Nickolas realized he stood directly in her path. Before he could even formulate a thought of stepping aside, she passed directly through him, filling every inch of his body with a soothing warmth, only to leave him cold as she continued past.

Shock and worry filled the faces of the crowd. Miss Castleton inquired after his well-being from directly beside him, as a fiancée ought, but Nickolas's attention remained riveted on Gwen. She had passed through the back wall of the ballroom and was headed, if his bearings were correct, directly toward The Tower.

"Something is not right, Nickolas." Dafydd's whisper barely penetrated his thoughts.

Frenzied conversations echoed all around. Only then did Nickolas truly look at his surroundings and discover his guests were waist-deep in a thick, eerie fog. Glancing out the windows, Nickolas could see the grounds of Tŷ Mynydd swathed in the same other-worldly haze.

Through the windows, he stared after Gwen. She was indeed making her way to The Tower, a lightness to her step that did not at all match her destination. Nickolas remembered all too well the feeling he'd fought on the stairwell of that tower. He could recall with perfect clarity the suffering on Gwen's face as she'd endured that place at his side.

"He should not have been here alone," she'd said. And she was doing just that. Going to The Tower. Alone.

A few of the guests were making their way out, thanking him for an enjoyable evening but claiming they were tired or had a long journey ahead of them. He knew, however, they were simply unnerved and were escaping. He was too concerned to do more than offer cursory adieus.

"Dafydd. Griffith."

"You're going after her," Griffith said, obviously not needing an explanation.

"I have to. She did as much for me."

His friends nodded. Nickolas pulled an overcoat on and cast aside his black mask.

"You will stand watch over the guests?" Nickolas asked them, buttoning his coat against the cold.

"Of course," Griffith said.

"Be careful, Nickolas." Dafydd spoke with almost unnerving somberness. "Gwen would not fear that place if there were not a very good reason."

He nodded and began his trek across the heavily fogged landscape.

"God keep you, Nickolas Pritchard," Dafydd's voice echoed after him.

"I certainly hope He does," Nickolas muttered to himself and trudged determinedly toward The Tower, which glowed brighter than he ever remembered seeing it.

Chapter Twenty-One

"Have you seen my father, Taffy?" Gwen asked, watching the man lug a bundle of swords down the long, narrow passage leading to the base of the east tower. She had not yet accustomed herself to living in a castle under siege. Her heart pounded at the thought of the army gathering across the meadow outside the castle walls.

"He's up to the east tower, Miss Gwenllian," Taffy replied. "In an odd mood, he is. Grumbling and stalking around."

Gwen nodded her understanding. The arrival of King Henry's troops had dampened everyone's spirits but had noticeably worried her usually unflappable father.

"He called out for me across the courtyard," Gwen said. "He did not sound put out with me this time."

"Then you'd best go find out what it is Master Cadoc wants," Taffy suggested. "Might be important."

Gwen agreed and continued her quick walk toward the tower. Everything seemed important these past forty-eight hours. Y Castell was in a constant state of agitated activity. Weapons were gathered and sharpened. Fortifications were reenforced. Gwen wondered at times if their efforts would do any good. They were vastly outnumbered.

But Father would scold her for such thinking. He had been insistent they would be victorious. Still, something lurked in the back of his eyes that worried her. Despite his confident words and demeanor, her father was afraid.

Gwen hurried her steps, hoping to prove something of a comfort to him. He would have some task or another for her to perform, and she would, as always, do it with enthusiasm and anxiety, hoping this time she would receive his full approval.

The bottom of the east tower teemed with activity. At least half of the castle's gathered population must have been wandering in and out of the single door and up and down the stairs to still other passageways and parts of the fortified castle walls. Gwen greeted them as she passed. The crowd's nervous solemnity made Gwen uneasy. She hated the thought of war but knew it lurked just outside the thick stone walls.

She noted as she looked around that none of those gathered there were among her closest associates. Seldom were *all* of her friends sleeping or on guard duty at the same time.

"Gwenllian."

She spun at the sound of Father's voice above her. He stood, the very model of a warrior, halfway up the flight of stairs leading to the tower room.

"I heard you calling for me, *Dadi.*" She forced a smile. She had the oddest feeling of foreboding. *Do not be absurd*, she silently scolded herself. Father did not appear angry or overset or worried. So why did her skin seem to suddenly crawl? "Is there something I can do for you?"

"As a matter of fact, there is," he replied, holding a hand out to her. "There is something you must do. For all of us."

It was a strange thing for him to say. Something that she *must* do? What did he mean? And for *all of us*. Everyone at Y Castell? That seemed unlikely, nigh near impossible, even.

Gwen walked to the stairwell and climbed, placing her fingers in the massive hand of her father. His hand closed around hers, and a deep, chilling shiver snaked down her spine. Gwen impulsively pulled back on her hand, intending to chafe at her cold arms, but her father's grip tightened.

"I am cold, Father."

"There is a fire built in the room. You will be warm enough."

He pulled her rather forcefully up the remaining stairs and led her through the door to the tower room. It had, over the hundred years since Y Castell had been built, served as a bedchamber and was still furnished as such. The large four-poster bed was hung with heavy, velvet curtains. A table and chairs occupied another portion of the room. In the fireplace, built directly into the wall, a fire crackled, but Gwen did not feel any warmer. She had the almost overwhelming urge to wrap her arms around herself the way she had as a child when a storm or a dream had frightened her. But Father had yet to release her hand. His grip, if anything, had tightened further.

Behind her, Gwen heard the door lock. She turned to see Arwyn ap Bedwyr, dressed in his usual priest's attire, slip the key into his pocket.

Gwen looked from her father to the priest, her heart pounding in her chest. The look the two men exchanged was heavy with unspoken meaning, and suddenly, she felt afraid.

Arwyn nodded to Gwen's father before turning and walking to the table. He lifted from its surface a length of deepest black fabric. Out the tower window visible to the awaiting invading army he unfurled it, securing the end he held to nails already driven into the stone along the bottom of the window.

A black flag? Gwen silently asked herself. *Why black? What does that mean?*

"Are you truly willing to do this, Cadoc?" The priest turned back to face them, looking piercingly at Gwen's father.

"We are both determined." Father seemed to be reminding the other man of a previously determined fact. "Y Castell must not fall into the hands of the enemy."

The priest nodded. "Then we will protect this land at all costs."

"At all costs," Gwen's father answered. His hand shifted to wrap around her wrist, his other hand doing the same with her other arm.

"*Dadi?*" Gwen whispered, her fear causing her voice to shake.

He ignored her plea, his eyes focused on Arwyn ap Bedwyr. Gwen watched the priest lift a heavy tome from the table and carry it slowly to a wooden lectern that Gwen had never before seen in that room. The book he carried was not a Bible, she knew immediately. As the priest opened the book, a warmth-stealing chill permeated the room.

"*Dadi!*" Gwen pled in anguish. She knew beyond a doubt that something horrible was about to happen if her father did not stop the priest.

But her father's reply was directed to the other man. "Begin."

*   *   *

The closer Nickolas came to The Tower, the stranger the night became. All around him, things and people began to materialize. Ghostly figures dressed in the style of centuries before—Gwen's time, he was certain— appeared, walking about, working in the open fields around him. Shadowy images of walls and buildings, tools and weapons took wispy form before his eyes. Only their slightly translucent appearance and the fact that Nickolas could walk through these visions indicated they were not real.

The Tower still stood as real and solid as it always had and glowed more bright by the moment. All around the sinister edifice, an eerie mist re-created the walls of Y Castell as they must have appeared on *Nos Galan Gaeaf* nearly four hundred years earlier. Serfs and knights, peasants and workers busied themselves in the courtyard.

The base of The Tower, where the heavy wooden door stood, was now enclosed in the phantom walls of the ancient castle. How solid had the illusions become? Could he simply walk through them?

"Where is the entrance to the castle?" Nickolas asked a passing specter, but he received no reaction, no response, no acknowledgment. They did not see or hear him, Nickolas realized. Just as Gwen had not.

Thoughts of Gwen pulled Nickolas's eyes to The Tower once more. He knew she had gone there. There had to be a way to get inside. He would not leave her there alone.

Then his gaze fell on a sight that sent chills through every inch of his body. A ghostly black flag hung ominously from a tower window. Nickolas remembered Dafydd's account all too well. The black flag was hung as a symbol of death, *Gwen's* death.

"No." Nickolas gasped. Never mind that Gwen was a ghost. Never mind that she could not die again. Desperate to reach her, he ran as fast as he could toward the ghostly castle walls.

"It is only an illusion," he told himself.

He slipped through the misty walls. Nickolas breathed a sigh of relief as he headed toward the outer door of The Tower. Among the phantom figures and ghostly walls, only Nickolas and that tower were physical. He couldn't simply slip through the heavy door as he had done with the illusionary barrier of Y Castell.

The Tower's outer door hadn't been locked when he'd spent the night inside. He prayed it would not be now.

He pulled the heavy door open. Its ghostly double did not budge. Nickolas slipped through the door of mist as easily as he had the phantom walls. The once-empty tower was furnished as it must have been the night Gwen died. Several anxious-looking men paced the floor. Everything and everyone inside the very real walls of the old tower was no more substantial than mist rising off a meadow at sunrise. The combination was eerie.

The ghostly figures around him wore solemn, tense expressions as they sharpened their weaponry. They were living in a castle under siege.

But where, he asked himself, was Gwen? Was she "alive"? Was he too late?

A crash like the sound of a chair being toppled echoed from above his head. All around him, the spirits of warriors long dead looked up to the source of the sound. They had heard it too. The sound, then, had occurred in the past. But he could hear it. Was he part of the scene playing out? No one seemed to see him there or notice his presence. Perhaps he was only a spectator, able to see and hear but do nothing. The idea sat cold and painful in his heart.

He knew where he had to go. Up the stairs to the room Gwen feared most. He instinctively knew she would be there. What place would hold more pain for any person than the room in which she had died?

Nickolas ran for the stairs only to be felled by the paralyzing coldness that permeated the narrow stairwell.

Nickolas pulled himself up one step at a time, fighting the freezing pain that hampered his every movement. He sent words of supplication heavenward with increasing frequency and intensity as he pushed closer to his goal. He would need divine intervention if he were to make it there.

He all but collapsed at the landing, cold sweat trickling down his forehead and between his shoulder blades. He shivered violently. The atmosphere beside the door was beyond cold—it was oppressive, grasping.

Nickolas leaned heavily against the wall in an attempt to regain his strength. Never had a simple flight of stairs so entirely exhausted him.

His own drained body was forgotten in the next moment when a voice, piercingly familiar, penetrated the closed door.

"Please, Father," the voice begged. "Please don't do this."

The words, he registered, were Welsh. He heard them not with his ears but almost as if with his very soul. And his soul, despite the limits of his brain, understood what was said. Even if the words had been completely uninterpretable, the tone and voice were unmistakable. Gwen was terrified.

Nickolas pounded on the door when he found it locked. He shouted to be permitted entrance. But as with the ghosts below him, his efforts had no noticeable effect. Both fists thudded repeatedly on the unyielding door.

"I cannot come this far and leave her in there to suffer," Nickolas pleaded in a frustrated and anguished whisper. "A locked door shouldn't—"

Locked door.

Good heavens! What was he pounding for? He had a key—a key hidden inside the statue that Gwen had sworn was erected in apology for whatever those two men had done just beyond the unyielding door.

"Stop! Please stop!"

Gwen's voice begged once more as Nickolas fumbled with the key, using what little strength he still possessed to push it into the ancient lock. With a squeal of protest, the lock turned. Nickolas shoved the door with his shoulder, and it flew open, though the ghostly door remained locked and shut, precisely as the outer door of The Tower had.

All around the room, heavy pieces of furniture and their exact duplicates in otherworldly form seemed to vie for the space they both occupied. The effect was dizzying, as though he were seeing double and could do nothing to realign the sight.

At a lectern in the middle of the room, the ghost of a priest—*that priest*, he was sure—read what sounded and felt like a curse, a spell of darkest, blackest magic, while across the room Gwen was held fast in the enormous arms of a man who, Nickolas knew from sheer deduction, was her father.

Her eyes were wide with terror as she struggled against him, but the man was twice her size. Dragging her across the room, despite her efforts at stopping him, was proving all too easy for him.

"You must do this, Gwenllian," her father barked, momentarily stopping the priest in his recitation. "Y Castell must be saved."

"Father, please." Tears choked Gwen's words. "I will fight alongside you. I will. I will defend Y Castell. But I do not wish to die this way. Please!"

Nickolas rushed to her side, intent on pulling her from her father's lethal embrace. But his arms simply passed through them both, doing nothing to free her from the anguish she was living. How many times had she been through this? Had she endured such terror three hundred ninety-eight times before? He closed his eyes against the horror of the thought, against his own impotence in the face of her suffering.

There had to be a way. There had to be something he could do, something to save her from enduring this once more. He now knew, based on her own words, that Gwen was going to die in that room, that very night, at the hands of her father and the priest. That, no doubt, was what they had done that had caused so much guilt—the evil act that still haunted The Tower. If Nickolas's impression of the priest's role was accurate, this was an attempt to protect their home with the worst sort of witchcraft.

Chapter Twenty-Two

"YOU WILL SERVE US FAR better this way than as an incompetent fighter," Gwen's father grumbled. "Now enough of your protest, child." He clamped a hand over her mouth. "'Tis an honor to defend one's home."

No sooner had the words left the ghostly man's mouth than he yelped out in pain and inadvertently released his captive. Gwen ran at full sprint to the door, tugging at the ring that served as a handle.

"It is open, Gwen!" Nickolas shouted to her, running to where she was struggling. The physical door was, indeed, open. But she, it seemed, could not pass through the still-locked ghostly barrier.

"She bit me," Gwen's father sputtered in shock.

Good for you, Nickolas silently saluted as he desperately tried to open the door for her. His hands simply passed through, touching nothing, changing nothing.

"The door is locked, Gwenllian," the priest told her, his voice calm, almost apologetic. "You must remain inside until this is finished."

"No." She spun around, facing them both.

Emotional pain like Nickolas had never experienced radiated through him at the expression in her eyes. It was stark and desperate fear.

"If it is such an honor to die for one's home"—she snapped her face toward her father—"then you do so. You allow your very soul to be traded for a pile of stone!"

"You will not defy me in this, girl," her father angrily retorted.

"Of course she will," the priest countered. "But time is short, and you must see that she is made to do her duty."

The priest stood in his position at the lectern as if delivering a sermon in church.

"How dare you!" Nickolas shouted at him, knowing he would make no impact but unable to hold his tongue. "You, a man of God, would mock Him this way!"

Be ye chastised and warned all ye who disregard the laws of God.

Those words took on weight. This priest, this fallen, despicable priest, had done more to violate God's commands than taking his own life. He'd taken the life of an innocent young lady and done so as part of a very ungodly ritual.

Gwen had returned to tugging at the door, no doubt her panic stealing her ability to realize the futility of her actions. Not ten steps away, her father tore a tablecloth into long, narrow strips.

The priest's voice began again, speaking words that chilled Nickolas to his bones. He and Gwen's father were offering up an innocent soul for the protection of dark forces, vowing to repeat the ritual throughout time in order to continue the protective state.

That, then, was the reason this was happening once more. They were, in their deaths, fulfilling their vows and forcing Gwen to do the same. Had they, Nickolas wondered fleetingly, returned to this place during their lifetimes as well? Returning to the scene of so much suffering and having to face again and again what they'd done to Gwen would have driven guilt into the coldest of hearts. Suicide probably had seemed a ready escape from such an obligation.

"Stop her!" the priest suddenly shouted.

Nickolas turned, along with Gwen's father, to see her climbing to the window. Laws! She hadn't jumped out, had she? Was that the reason she wasn't buried in the churchyard? She had, in desperation, killed herself?

But she was pulled roughly back inside by her father, her screams for help echoing through the room and, no doubt, into the courtyard below. Did no one hear? Nickolas ran to the window himself. Below, the ghosts of Gwen's long-ago friends, neighbors, servants, and associates talked to one another, occasionally looking up in confusion. They didn't understand? Or they did and were unwilling to help? Why did no one do anything?

"If you would cooperate, child, this would be far easier on us all."

Nickolas turned to see Gwen's father dragging her, though she struggled valiantly, to the bed.

"Cooperate?" Nickolas spat at him, furious. "You are killing your own child!"

And I can do nothing to help her.

The priest began again, and Nickolas wished with all his might he could simply strangle the man and stop his cruel words from killing Gwen. But Arwyn ap Bedwyr had accomplished his horrific curse nearly four hundred times over. What could Nickolas possibly do to change that now?

The fog that had followed Nickolas from the house began to crawl across the floor of The Tower room. To Nickolas's surprise, the priest took note of it, pausing long enough to glance at the swirling mist around his ankles.

"The rest is crucial, Cadoc," Arwyn said ominously. "There is but one chance. Midnight is nearly upon us."

Cadoc nodded and, still cruelly clasping his daughter to him, reached up and yanked back the heavy curtains surrounding the chamber's bed. The physical curtains, those existing in Nickolas's time and sphere, moved as well.

Cadoc pushed Gwen toward the bed. "I hadn't intended to tie you down, Gwenllian, but you leave me with no other choice. You knocked over a chair rather than sat in it. You bit your own father—"

"Who is attempting to kill me!" Gwen shot back.

Same Gwen, Nickolas thought fleetingly. She was no wilting flower to accept her lot meekly.

All feelings of pride in her fire and bravery fled from Nickolas's mind as he realized the next truth: Gwen's father, Cadoc, intended to tie her to the bed so she couldn't flee. Which meant she had died on that bed. Everything else, he realized, looking around at the now both physical and ghostly items in the room, had remained where they were after Gwen's death.

Gwen—his breath caught in his throat at the thought—would have too.

She wasn't buried in the courtyard because she hadn't been buried at all. Nickolas knew that she had been left, tied down, on that very bed. There would be little left after four hundred years, but the thought that she had been given such an undignified final rest was sickening. Despite the sudden nausea he felt, Nickolas's eyes turned toward the bed where the curtains were pulled back.

His heart lurched to a halt when he saw, clearly defined, the silhouette of a young lady lying deathly still on the bed. This was no skeleton, neither was it a ghostly illusion, for Gwen the specter was being pushed by her father at the very edge of the bed.

Nickolas moved to the side of the bed, opposite where Gwen and her father, in ghostly form, struggled. He stared in awe at a lady he recognized in an instant. She looked as though she had only just fallen asleep. Nothing in her coloring or countenance suggested that she was dead, though Nickolas knew she was. Her eyes were closed, but her expression was one of surprise, as if caught off guard by the suddenness of her departure. At least he saw no pain written on her features.

Nickolas stood in shock, struggling to comprehend what he saw. Cadoc managed to toss his daughter onto the bed, securing her there with ties. Gwen, the ghost, lay captive in the same space occupied by her perfectly preserved body.

All around him, the physical objects and their ghostly counterparts seemed to melt together, no longer giving the illusion of seeing double. The door, the actual, physical, present-day door, slammed shut, melting into the ghostly door. If the ancient door, made of fog and memories, was locked, was the physical door now locked as well? The phantom furnishings, walls, even the book from which the priest read, melded with their present-day selves. Only the ghosts remained misty whispers.

"Continue, Arwyn."

Nickolas hadn't even realized the priest had stopped his droning. He knew, felt it in his soul, that if the priest concluded his ceremony, this ghostly Gwen would die once more. And he would be forced to watch with no means of helping her.

He ran to the window, prepared to shout for the crowd below to save Gwen, hoping they would hear him this time. But they had vanished. Indeed, the ghostly remnants of the castle had vanished, and the fog had dissipated. All that remained of the night's horrors was concentrated in the room in which he stood, a melding of the physical remnants of that horrible night and their ghostly doubles.

He rushed back to Gwen's side, knowing he could do nothing but needing to feel he had at least not abandoned her. But she had changed. Just as the furniture and the door had enveloped their fifteenth-century remnants, the reposed body of Gwen had completely absorbed the ghostly figure of her.

The sleeping lady was awake, struggling against the very real bonds that held her captive. She was there *physically*, in living form, not simply as a wisp of spirit.

"Please, *Father*." Her voice sounded in his ears in indiscernible Welsh and echoed in his soul in words he understood.

"Gwen?" Nickolas whispered, his voice breathy in his confusion and shock. She did not answer, did not acknowledge his words. A barrier yet separated them, one he did not know how to bridge.

Nickolas reached out and laid his hand on top of hers, fisted as she struggled against the bonds. His fingers met flesh. She was real! Something in her expression changed, as if she had felt his touch as something little more than a whisper.

He would not leave her so helpless. She might not be completely aware of him, but she was there, physically. She was frightened and very much in danger. Nickolas yanked at the linen bonds, fumbling to untie them. Gwen's eyes shot to the strips of fabric. So did Cadoc's.

Cadoc swore. "They're untying."

"What?" Arwyn jumped, rushing to the bedside and staring.

Gwen had begun tugging, trying to set herself free, not realizing that she made his task harder. If he could loose her, would she be able to free herself from the rest? Could she get away?

"Retie her," Arwyn insisted. "Use more strips. We have only minutes, Cadoc. Minutes. The future of Y Castell depends on this."

"You will not hurt her again!" Nickolas shouted as he pulled desperately at the bonds. "I will not allow it!"

He had one hand free in that moment. Afraid her captors would simply grab it and pull her away, Nickolas took her wrist in his hand, momentarily shocked to feel a pulse thrumming inside, and climbed over her, across the bed to where her other arm was tied down.

"Only a few moments, Gwen," Nickolas reassured her, knowing she could not hear him. "I will have you free in a moment."

Then he heard Gwen's tiny voice, choked with emotion and confusion, whispering words that strengthened his own resolve.

"The Lord is my shepherd," she began the familiar psalm. "I shall not want."

"Stop!" the priest snapped, anxiety written in his features. "You cannot invoke scripture at a time like this."

"He maketh me to lie down in green pastures." Nickolas joined his voice to hers as he pulled determinedly at the strip of cloth keeping her captive yet. His English melded with her Welsh, and yet, the words were the same. Silently, Nickolas pleaded with her to continue. He hoped the words would give her courage the same as they were giving him.

Both ghostly men grabbed at Gwen's arm, at the ties Nickolas was unknotting, but their hands of mist were unable to grasp what was real and solid. He kept her free hand tightly locked in his own, attempting to untie the other bond with his remaining hand. He had a horrifying suspicion that if he let go of her arm, those men would somehow be able to take hold of her again.

"You must finish before she can escape!" Cadoc barked at the priest.

Arwyn moved quickly back to the lectern, pausing a moment as he searched the open page in front of him for his place in the curse.

They are going to finish. The terrifying thought rushed through Nickolas's mind. If he didn't get her out, they would finish. For only a second, he contemplated leaving Gwen to go after the priest, unsure what he would or could do to stop the man. But her continued recitation of the well-known psalm faltered as fear choked her voice.

"I am here, Gwen." If only she could hear him! He turned his attention back to his task. As he was, she at least knew some unseen force was helping her, that she was not alone.

"Help me!" Nickolas pleaded with the heavens. He could not save her on his own.

Prayers, he discovered, were sometimes answered with alarming speed and precision. A swift, hard knock on the door was immediately followed by Dafydd's voice. "Nickolas!" He sounded anxious. "Nickolas, are you all right? I heard you shouting. What—"

"Help me, Dafydd!" Nickolas bellowed back.

"The door is locked." That was Griffith's voice. They'd both come.

Nickolas heard them shake the uncooperative barrier.

The key. Where was—? "I left the key in the door," Nickolas shouted. It was, no doubt, too dark to see without the eerie glow and ghostly fire that lit the inside of the room.

Nickolas continued his struggle. What kind of blasted, stupid knot had the man used? Gwen grew unnervingly silent as the priest continued his relentless, dark destruction. She no longer moved, no longer struggled. He couldn't be certain she even breathed. Was the curse already taking effect? Was she dying all over again?

"Stay with me, Gwen!"

The door flew open.

Chapter Twenty-Three

GRIFFITH STUMBLED INSIDE, CLEARLY HAVING shoved the door open. Dafydd, pale and trembling in the doorway, stared in shocked disbelief at the sight that met his eyes. They'd come through the bone-chilling atmosphere of the stairwell and walked unsuspectingly into this scene of terror.

"Stop him!" Nickolas barked out, pointing at the priest.

"That isn't scripture." Dafydd stared at the ghostly priest.

"Get the book!" Nickolas shouted. He nearly had the knot undone but wasn't entirely sure that simply getting Gwen out would stop the curse. Nor did he know if he had time to even cross the room. "Get the book! He must not be permitted to finish!"

At a wobbly run, Griffith lunged at the lectern, thrusting his shoulder against it. The entire thing, book and all, crashed to the floor.

Dafydd grabbed the book.

"The fire!" Nickolas shouted as he managed to finally untie the bind around Gwen's wrist.

He jumped off the bed and scooped Gwen's limp, unmoving body into his arms. Dafydd lifted the heavy tome and threw it into the roaring ghostly fire with so much force Nickolas half expected it would simply fly through the thick stone wall.

An anguished cry filled the air as the book exploded in the flames. The fog in the room rose, swirling around them in a wind so stiff Nickolas couldn't keep his footing. He dropped to his knees, cradling Gwen against him. He inched toward the center of the room, where the wind was calm, like the eye of a storm.

Nickolas glanced down at Gwen, so still and fragile in his arms and yet so very real. He gently touched her face. How he wished she could see him, could talk to him, could tell him she was well. But she didn't move, didn't open her eyes.

A sudden gust of downward wind nearly knocked Nickolas flat. He braced himself against it, refusing to release Gwen. Looking up, he watched as what little furniture had escaped the swirling whirlwind divided itself once more into the real and the apparition. All the ghostly elements in the room were fading, and fading quickly.

Nickolas looked down at Gwen. Would he lose her too? Was she about to fade into nothingness?

"I love you, Gwen," Nickolas whispered, holding her fiercely. "I love you."

He kissed her gently on her unmoving mouth, pulling her tighter into his embrace. He fought back a stinging in his throat and the threat of tears in his eyes. He knew, somehow, that breaking the cycle of that spell had released the hold it had had on Gwen. She was free. He very much feared it meant she would leave him.

The fog around him dissipated, the wind died down to stillness. Nickolas remained where he was, holding Gwen to him. Every last evidence of the night's ordeal had disappeared. Every ghost had faded into nothingness.

Images of all that had happened, the horror he'd witnessed, flashed mercilessly through his mind. He had to forcibly shut out the reminder that Gwen had lived through the terrifying events of that night hundreds of times. Only during this last experience had she been saved from it. It was his one source of consolation: he had saved her, even if it meant losing her for good.

He would have to return to the house knowing she would never again haunt its corridors. Her room, he was certain, would feel empty and cold without her presence. The entire house would.

"This is what they did," Dafydd whispered from across the room. "Black magic of the worst kind."

Nickolas actually jumped. He'd forgotten about Dafydd and Griffith. They both sat across the room, pale and clearly shaken. Griffith rubbed at the shoulder he'd heaved into the thick, wooden lectern. His eyes darted about, shock sitting heavy in his expression. Nickolas pulled himself together enough to speak. "They sacrificed Gwen for the sake of a 'pile of stone.'"

"Disregarded the laws of God," Dafydd said weakly.

"*Disregarded*? No. They were *violating* the laws of God. A pact with the devil."

Nickolas stroked Gwen's hair, trying not to think about the fact that she was gone just as all the others connected to the night's horrors were gone.

"It was Latin." Dafydd rose to his feet with some difficulty; what he'd seen and experienced had obviously deeply affected him. "The priest's words. They were sacrificing her life for . . . for preservation. Nothing in this room should have remained intact as long as it has. The curse preserved it all."

Preserved it all. Including Gwen. Nickolas looked down into her beloved face one last time, determined to memorize it just as she looked then. Her face was rosy and real, not the pale, ghostly imitation he'd only ever seen before. Her hair shone a vivid shade of red.

So close! He'd come so close!

"At least now she can be properly buried." Griffith's tone indicated he knew the thought was hardly comforting.

"She deserves that." Nickolas brushed his fingers once more along her soft cheek and followed the line of her jaw, resting his fingers gently on her neck. "No one, let alone a lady, should have to endure what—"

He stopped. Immediately.

"What is it?" Dafydd asked, still leaning against the wall for support.

Nickolas pressed his fingers harder against the side of her neck. "Gwen?" he asked, anxiously, desperately. He had felt a pulse. "Gwen!"

"Good heavens! She's alive?" Dafydd crossed toward them but stopped in shock when Gwen began to move. "How is this possible?"

Griffith struggled to his feet as well. "She must have still been alive when the curse was broken, her body and soul still united." He stood leaning against the wall. "You broke the curse in time."

"Gwen?" Nickolas tried again.

She stirred only slightly, as if her limbs were too heavy and stiff to be maneuvered.

"Oh, Gwen," Nickolas whispered, hardly able to speak for astonished joy. She lived!

She was still lying in his arms when her eyes flew open. Deep-brown eyes, Nickolas noted. Brown and beautiful and, he realized with a jolt, completely and utterly terrified.

He tightened his hold on her to offer support. Was she still reeling from the ordeal with her father?

She struggled against him, her eyes wide with fear and focused on his face. Unable to tolerate holding her captive when she only just escaped such a situation, Nickolas released her. He could offer reassurance verbally, from a slight distance if necessary.

There was no softening in her eyes, no relieving recognition. In fact, she scooted across the floor, farther distancing herself from him. She looked like a frightened fox cornered by a pack of hounds. Gwen spoke, but not in English.

Griffith's eyes grew wide at whatever it was she'd said.

"She asked, 'Who are you?'" Dafydd interpreted, sounding as surprised as Nickolas was by the question.

"Who am I?" Nickolas gaped. "I am Nickolas, Gwen."

"*Sais,*" she whispered, her tone obviously one of confusion.

"*Englishman,*" Dafydd translated again. He spoke directly to Gwen in Welsh. Nickolas knew for certain then that the spell had been broken. Unlike before when he had instinctively understood both Welsh and Latin, he was now completely at a loss.

Griffith joined in their rushed and frantic conversation. Nickolas's eyes jumped between them. He had no idea what was being said. Gwen motioned to him more than once, uncertainty and fear in her expression.

Gwen pulled herself to her feet, but her legs faltered. When Nickolas moved to help her, she darted away from him, the frightened look in her eyes seeming to grow by the minute. She moved anxiously to the window and looked out then turned back to face the room. Her face had gone nearly as white as it had been during her time as a specter.

Her eyes, those beautiful, haunting eyes, turned to Nickolas, simultaneously pleading and accusing. "Where are your fellow Englishmen?" she asked in heavily accented English. "Where are the soldiers?"

"There are no soldiers here," Nickolas answered, baffled.

Her brows drew closer in a look of overwhelming confusion. She turned back to the window, threw open the heavy leaded glass, and put her head out into the cold, dark night. "It is gone," she said. "Y Castell is gone."

Again, Dafydd spoke to her in the Welsh Nickolas increasingly wished he knew. Gwen turned to look at Dafydd, tears beginning to well up in her eyes. Nickolas had never once seen her cry. He discovered in that moment that the sight was painful for him to watch. He instinctively reached out for her again, needing the reassurance of her in his arms.

She jerked out of his reach, throwing Welsh words at him, words that did not feel welcoming in the least.

Griffith spoke to her again. His tone was precisely what one would expect to hear from a person trying to calm another in the face of overwhelming worry.

She shook her head at whatever Griffith had said. Her eyes shot around the room, and Nickolas saw her shiver. He moved toward her, ready to wrap her in his warm embrace, to whisper words of reassurance, to offer her his strength and support. But again, she moved swiftly away from him. She backed toward the door, her eyes snapping between him and the other two men, her look one of alarm and confusion.

Gwen turned, her skirts swirling around her, and fled the room. Nickolas was certain he heard her call out for taffy.

"Taffy?" he asked, perplexed, bewildered, feeling alone and very confused.

"It is an old Welsh nickname," Griffith said. "I believe she is searching for her friends."

"What?"

"She doesn't remember, Nickolas," Dafydd said. "She doesn't remember any of it. She thought you were one of King Henry's soldiers. She thought that Y Castell still stood. In her mind it is yet four hundred years ago."

"She doesn't remember anything that happened while she was a ghost?" Nickolas asked, his stomach knotting.

"It doesn't seem so. She didn't recognize any of us, nor understand what had happened to the walls of her home. She found our odd style of dress almost as alarming as the rest."

"She doesn't remember me," Nickolas whispered, the realization painful.

"I'd best follow her." Dafydd moved toward the door. "She is frightened and lost. She will need—"

"I will go after her," Nickolas insisted.

"Nickolas." Griffith stopped him with a firm grip on his arm. "*You* have a fiancée waiting at the house. A gentleman who is engaged to one young lady cannot go haring off after another. Let Dafydd go after Gwen."

It was like a dash of cold water. His love lived, truly lived. And he was promised to another. He could not, with any degree of honor, back out of the engagement. And he could not, without utterly disrespecting his future wife, see to Gwen's welfare. That would, by necessity, be left to Dafydd.

"Come along, Nickolas." Griffith urged him out of the room after Dafydd had gone. "No need to stay here torturing yourself."

They took the steps slowly, both of them faltering.

Griffith kept at Nickolas's side as they left The Tower behind. The atmosphere, Nickolas noticed, with what little of his brain still functioned, had grown less oppressive, less frigid, less *evil*. The grip the centuries-old curse had over The Tower was gone. It was over.

And yet, there wasn't the happy ending he had wanted. "She didn't remember me."

Griffith had no soothing words to offer as they step-by-step made their way toward the house.

"And she was afraid of me." That hurt even more than the lack of recognition. There'd been something like hatred in Gwen's eyes.

"You are a *Sais*, Nickolas. An Englishman. In her time, there was ample reason to fear your countrymen, ample reason to despise them, even."

His heart dropped. "But I love her."

Griffith gave him a look of empathy. "I know. You may have to resign yourself to being grateful she is alive, even if you must be a stranger to her. If she never regains the past four hundred years of memories, she might never allow you near her."

He *did* rejoice for Gwen. She lived and had escaped the cruel machinations of her father and the priest. But in giving her that gift, he'd lost her. The woman he loved saw him as nothing more than a sworn enemy. She might never learn to forgive him. Even in his relief at her release, he felt utterly desolate.

* * *

Nickolas awoke near dinnertime the next evening. He'd returned to the house exhausted and physically spent. He had gone to his rooms by way of Gwen's but allowed himself only a fleeting glimpse. He knew if he went inside, the weight of all that had happened, the feeling of loss, would overwhelm him. He would simply collapse in there, unable to summon the strength, physically or mentally, to leave her place of solace and refuge.

He had reached his bed and fallen on top of it, fully clothed, and slipped into a fitful sleep. Again and again, the night's events replayed in his dreams. He felt Gwen in his arms once more, relived that moment of euphoria when he realized she was alive, that he hadn't lost her after all, only to come crashing back to the moment she fled.

He dressed with care and shaved before making his way with reluctant determination to the drawing room to face his guests. There was much they would need and want to know. He would do his best to tell them what he could. He decided before entering the room that he would not tell all. Mr. Castleton, at the very least, could be counted on to dog Gwen's heels if he knew a *former* ghost, something Nickolas doubted anyone had ever heard of, was in the vicinity. He would have to tell them something though. Nickolas wished he'd thought to consult Dafydd and Griffith first so they could concoct the same story.

He came across Griffith not long after emerging from his room. Did he look half as tired as Griffith did?

"I wondered if we'd see you at all today," Griffith said. "How are you getting on?"

"Terribly." But he managed a halfhearted smile.

Griffith walked with him a pace or two. "I spoke with Dafydd this morning."

"And?" Nickolas was anxious for news of Gwen.

"He is busy with a houseguest at the moment." The comment was pointed enough to be clear. Dafydd had found Gwen, and she was safe at the vicarage.

Nickolas breathed a sigh of relief as that weight lifted from his mind. "How is his houseguest adapting to . . . everything?"

"He said she is overwhelmed and confused."

Poor Gwen.

"But he also told me she seems less terrified. She is coming to trust him a little."

Gwen was learning to trust Dafydd, but could she ever trust him, an Englishman like those who'd attacked her home? If she never remembered him, would she give him a chance to show her he was different?

"I thought you would like to know she was safe," Griffith added.

Nickolas nodded and thanked him.

"For what it's worth to you," Griffith said, "I'm holding out hope that everything will work out for the best."

"I am attempting to do the same."

Griffith tipped him a laughing smile. "This *is* Wales. Extraordinary things happen here every day."

Nickolas was grateful for the reason to smile, if only briefly. He felt minimally better as he continued, alone, down the corridor.

Several doors before the drawing room, the sound of quiet weeping caught his attention. He peered inside the room and saw, to his surprise, Miss Castleton with her head in her hands, her shoulders shaking with sobs.

"Miss Castleton?" he asked, disturbed by her obvious suffering. He may not have felt a passionate love for the young lady, but he did care about her feelings.

She looked up at him. Nickolas could see this was no minor distress. She had the look of one who was weeping her very heart out.

"Oh, Mr. Pritchard!"

Nickolas crossed to where she sat wringing a thoroughly drenched lacy handkerchief. He offered her one of his larger, more utilitarian squares of linen. "What has upset you, Miss Castleton?" he asked, disturbed by the sudden realization that he was not entirely sure what her first name was. Carol? Charlotte?

"Forgive me, sir. I am not usually such a . . . a . . . goose!" She looked nearly exasperated with herself, the tiniest bit of amusement showing through her obvious distress.

Nickolas had to smile at that. She was showing a little backbone, something she did not always do.

"It is only that . . . that . . ." She sniffled. Nickolas very much feared the floodgates were about to open once more. "He didn't come back when you did. He hasn't been here at all today. I am so worried that he is hurt or ill or upset. It isn't like him to not even send his regrets when he doesn't join us."

Nickolas tried to make sense of the rambling explanation. "*He?*"

"Dafydd," she cried. "You look so very worn out after whatever happened last night. What if he, too, is suffering? He is there all alone with no one to look out for him. His cook scarcely counts. She doesn't love him the way—"

She stopped so suddenly and turned so ridiculously red that Nickolas had no difficulty finishing her sentence on his own. Miss Castleton was in love with Dafydd. Just as Nickolas was in love with Gwen. So why in heaven's name were they marrying each other?

Further speculation brought a second realization crashing in on him. Dafydd had been withdrawn and unhappy ever since Nickolas's engagement to Miss Castleton. Hadn't the vicar left rather abruptly the night of the announcement? Those two had spent a great deal of time together previous to the betrothal and almost none since, though Nickolas could recall both glancing in the other's direction repeatedly whenever they were in company.

"Miss Castleton." He squared his shoulders and rose from the sofa. "Will you accompany me on a short walk?"

She nodded but looked nervous. What woman wouldn't be anxious to face a fiancé to whom she had very nearly blurted out her love for another man?

The butler and Miss Castleton's abigail were duly summoned, Miss Castleton clothed against the cold outdoors, and a message dispatched to Mr. and Mrs. Castleton that their daughter and her intended were going for a quick turn about the grounds.

A few minutes later, Nickolas knocked quite anxiously on the door of the vicarage.

Chapter Twenty-Four

"Mr. Pritchard," Miss Castleton anxiously whispered. "Oh, why have you brought me here?"

"You may thank me prettily at the end of the evening, Miss Castleton. I am about to save all of us from misery."

"I—"

Whatever response she might have made was cut off when Dafydd himself opened the door. His words were likewise muted when his eyes fell on Miss Castleton. The look of love reflected in both pairs of eyes made Nickolas roll his own at their collective stupidity.

"We have all been deucedly foolish," Nickolas declared, pushing past Dafydd and into the warm confines of the tidy vicarage. "Do not leave the poor lady out in the cold," Nickolas chastised when he noticed Dafydd remained frozen in place, looking longingly into the eyes of the lady he obviously adored.

Dafydd seemed to remember himself then and ushered her inside. "I really ought to reprimand you for your language," Dafydd said to Nickolas.

"You being the staid vicar and all?" Nickolas raised an ironic eyebrow.

"Precisely." Dafydd almost smiled. "But I confess my curiosity has overcome my better judgment, and I am simply going to ask you what this is all about."

"Miss Castleton is in desperate need of rescuing." The knowledge that he was about to escape what would probably have been a relatively happy marriage to a kind and good lady proved surprisingly uplifting.

"Rescuing?" The look of concern that instantly entered Dafydd's eyes removed every last doubt Nickolas had.

"She is on the verge of being whisked off to a life of utter misery at the hands of a man who neither deserves her nor adequately appreciates her."

Dafydd looked amusedly confused. Miss Castleton simply looked confused.

"It is up to you to save her, Dafydd, and up to her to allow herself to be saved. I, of course, am far too much of a gentleman to contemplate anything so vulgar as backing out of an obligation."

"Save her?"

"You are aggravatingly slow this evening, Dafydd. Sweep the poor damsel off her feet and save her from a fate worse than death. I am perfectly ready to be heartlessly jilted."

Sudden understanding dawned in Miss Castleton's eyes. Her expression grew unmistakably hopeful as she looked up at Dafydd, who was smiling rather triumphantly. He snaked an arm around Miss Castleton in a move so smoothly possessive Nickolas couldn't help but be impressed.

"I will leave you two to work out the details of your daring deed," Nickolas said, feeling more like himself than he had in some time.

"Wait, Nickolas." Dafydd stopped him before he'd even moved. "While I . . . um . . ." He cleared his throat and even blushed a little. Nickolas actually laughed out loud. "What I am trying to say is, would you be the superbly mannered gentleman I know you to be and see if my guest, in the *back sitting room*, is in need of anything?"

Instantly, Nickolas was on the alert. He knew the hinting look in Dafydd's eyes. He left the soon-to-be-engaged couple and moved swiftly toward the back of the vicarage. His steps, however, slowed as he approached the door.

She likely wouldn't recognize him, might even be afraid of him still.

But a thought registered in the very next instant. He was free! Just as she was. If he had to court her all over again, he would be more than willing. He would be happy to, in fact. He simply must determine his behavior by following her lead. If she was skittish, he would go slowly. If she was feeling more herself, he could flirt and tease and compliment as he had before. How he hoped for the latter, for both their sakes.

Nickolas knocked on the door. Welsh words he hoped meant "come in" answered. He slowly opened the door, shutting it softly behind him as he stepped inside. His eyes found Gwen at the window.

Her hair hung loosely behind her, cascading in waves of deepest red. Dafydd had somehow managed to procure her a new gown in an awe-inspiring shade of green. He moved quietly to where she stood, still gazing out at a view of Tŷ Mynydd in the distance.

"Hello, Gwen," he said softly.

She looked up at him. Nickolas's breath caught in his lungs. Gads, she was beautiful. Stunning. And completely confused.

"I think I should know you," she whispered in English and shook her head. "But I can't . . . quite . . ." Her eyes returned to the scenery lit by the last traces of sunset. "It is all very frustrating."

"I would imagine so." He laid his hand slowly on top of hers, giving her time to pull away if she wished. But her hand remained in his, a frisson of awareness passing upward through his arm at the contact he'd tried to achieve so many times without being able to. "Do you remember nothing?"

"Very little," she said. "Only snatches here and there."

"And Dafydd, er—" She did know that was his name, didn't she?

"My host," Gwen finished for him.

"Yes. Has he explained any of this to you?"

"He has tried."

She looked up at him once more. It was all Nickolas could do to keep from folding her in his arms and kissing that sweet little mouth. But as she still didn't know him from Adam, it hardly seemed the time.

"He informed me that I was dead for nearly four hundred years and had terrorized the neighborhood quite mercilessly. I am further informed that this is the year 1805, the King is quite irretrievably mad, the country is at war with France—something that is not difficult to believe—and that Wales is, and has been for some time, quite decidedly reconciled with England." She took a deep, obviously fortifying breath. "It is a great deal to take in at one time."

"I can understand that." Nickolas felt his smile growing. This was his Gwen. So determined in the face of adversity.

"But then, he also told me he is the vicar, which I have a very difficult time believing. I keep seeing him, in my mind, as a little boy quite happily disrupting Sunday services." Gwen shrugged. "He says he finds my selective memory very lowering."

Nickolas laughed. Yes. This was his Gwen.

Something in his laugh caught her attention, and she turned to fully face him. "I *do* know you," she said, though her brow was still furrowed with confusion. "But I don't remember how."

"Allow me to replenish that unreliable memory of yours," Nickolas said, pleased to see a smile growing on her lips. "I, whom you have more than once denounced for being too English, inherited Tŷ Mynydd from a distant cousin and came here with every intention of living the boring and uneventful life of a typical landowner. This would have been quite easily accomplished, except I soon found that my home housed a most mischievous and vexing ghost."

"*Mischievous and vexing?*" Gwen said, a teasing aspect to her tone. "That does not sound like anyone I remember."

But do you remember me? he silently wondered. "You declared war on my entire household, I will have you know. Going so far as to take possession of the pianoforte to pound out—"

"A Welsh battle anthem," Gwen finished for him, obviously surprised that she remembered.

"Precisely. But then my charm and wit won you over, and we stopped being enemies."

"Did we?" She watched him closely. Nickolas fervently hoped she had begun to remember him.

"You forgave my tendencies to be English and to misspell my last name, and I forgave your tendency to terrorize my houseguests," Nickolas added.

"Especially the one who stared at me all the time," Gwen said almost to herself, her gaze returning to the window.

"Especially him. And I was forever finding you gazing out of windows."

Again, she spun to face him. "You've said that before."

Nickolas nodded.

"And you do not speak Welsh," she added.

"Sadly, no. Though you told me, once upon a time, that you might be able to forgive that flaw in me, especially in light of the fact that my ancestry could be traced back to good Welsh stock. One could, you decided, simply overlook the other side of my family."

Her eyes narrowed in concentration. He could feel her studying him. Nickolas squeezed her hand, still held in his own, willing her to remember him. He would court her for as long as it took, but he was praying for a quick resolution. Patience did not come easily when all he wished to do was hold her and kiss her as he never could before.

Gwen's eyes dropped to the hand holding her own. She studied it as intently as she had his face. Her other hand lightly touched the back of his, her fingers running along the barely visible scars that ran the length of it.

"The dragon turned out to be a cat," she whispered. "Thus ended your career as a valiant knight."

"Yes, Gwen." She remembered the story he'd told her. He himself only recalled having done so because she mentioned it.

Her face turned back up to his, her eyes wide with something akin to amazement. Quite suddenly, there were tears in her eyes. He braced himself. She was crying. What had he done?

"Nickolas," she whispered.

His arms were around her so fast Nickolas wasn't sure she realized what had happened. "Oh, my darling," he breathed against her hair. "Please say you remember me now."

"Nickolas." She simply repeated the whispered name.

He held her tighter, his hands reveling in the solidity of her. He listened to each breath she took, memorized the unique flowerlike scent of her hair. *My Gwen*, he repeated over and over in his mind. She was real, and she was in his arms.

Gwen suddenly stiffened, and Nickolas felt himself panic. "Gwen?"

"Oh, Nickolas," she said, her tone one of absolute sorrow. "You . . . You are . . ."

"What is it, Gwen?" He reached out and stroked her cheek, but she pulled farther back.

"You are engaged," she said, her face suddenly very pale again. "I only just remembered, or I never would have . . . I would not have . . ." Where she had been pale a moment before, she was now blushing quite adorably.

"Would not have flung yourself at me?"

"*Flung myself?*" Oh, she hadn't lost any of her fire, that was for sure and certain. Obviously, his descriptive verb choice didn't meet with her approval. Nickolas very nearly laughed in awed amazement at the spark in her eyes. Heavens, he loved this woman! "I have never flung myself at a man in all my life . . . or death, for that matter. I will have you know, I—"

Her words of chastisement were abruptly and pleasantly cut off by the simple act of placing his fingers lightly over her lips. His blood pumped fast in his veins.

"Have a little sympathy, my dear," Nickolas said. "I have only just been quite cruelly jilted. I am not certain I will ever recover from the shock. Could you not be a little more sympathetic? Soothe my battered soul or something of that nature?"

"*Jilted?*" she said from beneath his word-muffling fingers.

"Most cruelly." Nickolas shook his head as if shocked by what had occurred. He allowed his hand to drift along her jaw, slide below her ear, and come to a rest at the back of her neck. His other hand slid around her waist, drawing her closer to him. "I am in sore need of consolation."

"Miss Castleton really did release you from your engagement?" Gwen closed her eyes, breathing less steadily than before. He found it quite gratifying to see that she was not indifferent to his touch.

"She is going to marry the vicar," Nickolas said, lightly pressing his lips to her forehead as he spoke. It wasn't a kiss but affected him deeply enough that it might have been. Part of him refused to believe he actually held her in his arms. Only twenty-four hours earlier, such a thing would have been impossible to even imagine. "And I am going to marry the ghost."

He heard and felt her intake of breath. "You are?" she whispered.

He moved his lips, still lightly touching her face, from her forehead, down the length of her nose, and kissed the tip of it. "I am," he said, his lips hovering over hers.

"Don't you think you ought to ask her first?"

Still a mere inch from kissing her, Nickolas grinned. He stepped back enough to look into her beautiful, deep-brown eyes. He took her hand in his. "Gwenllian ferch Cadoc ap Richard—"

"Oh, Nickolas," she said, wincing, "that was horrible. I barely even recognized that as my name."

"Perhaps I should stick with *my dearest love*," Nickolas suggested.

"I do like that." She smiled almost dreamily.

"Then, my dearest love"—he pressed her hand to his heart, holding it there with his own hand—"will you marry me and love me all of our lives? Will you teach me to speak Welsh and rid me of my horrible tendency to be very, very English? Will you allow me to simply hold your hand every single day so I can be certain you are truly real? Say yes, Gwen. Make me the most fortunate and excessively happy man in all the world."

Her eyes grew a little misty. "I do love you, Nickolas," she whispered, her smile gentle and loving. "Of course I will marry you and gladly do all those other things. Though I am not certain I am capable of the miracle of teaching you Welsh without your *English tendencies* destroying the entire thing."

"Aggravating wench." He laughed, pulling her to him once more. "That mouth of yours has been torturing me from the moment I first saw you."

"I do have a tendency to speak my mind." Gwen shrugged inside his embrace.

"Oh, it has very little to do with talking, I assure you."

Her little gasp of surprise was completely absorbed by his mouth pressing hungrily to her own. The horrors of the night before were set aside for the time. The weight of separation that had hung so heavily on him for weeks lifted. The world around them disappeared until all that remained was the feel of her in his arms, the sweetness of a kiss so long hoped for but so seemingly impossible, and the promise of a love that would endure across time.

Epilogue

October 31, 1806

It isn't every day a grand estate, widely reputed to be haunted, hosts an enormous festival and ball on *Nos Galan Gaeaf*. Scores of people claimed to have seen *Y Ladi Wen*, herself, at the previous year's gathering, despite only a handful of guests having been present at the time. The local population had conceived of the idea of a recurrent celebration, encouraged in their plan by the mistress of that very estate. Such a festival was sure to bring travelers and their overly plump pocketbooks from all over the kingdom. The idea had worked marvelously.

Overawed individuals followed the outline of the ancient walls of Y Castell, delineated by a line of carefully laid stones, and ended their guided penny-a-piece tour at a small monument.

"This monument marks the place where the east tower of Y Castell once stood. May all who stand in its ghostly shadow remember what was done here," the monument declared in both English and Welsh.

Speculation was rife as to what precisely was "done here." The carefully scripted tour guide speculated that during the brief Welsh uprising, a young man's act of bravery and love saved the life of an innocent young lady. Though, he assured them with the appropriate look of sorrow, such things could not be confirmed. For a vicar, the man was a decidedly good actor.

Elsewhere on the sprawling estate, revelers paused before a painting hung in a place of honor above the fireplace in the drawing room. Speculation as to the talented artist was rife, though all agreed it was surely the work of a master. The subject matter could not be mistaken. There, come to life on canvas, was Y Castell bathed in the colors of spring.

Whilst the visitors, who were rather unabashedly hoping to be scared out of their wits, rambled the estate, purchasing wares from local craftsmen and generally making life economically better for many a Welshman, the vicar, finished with the day's tours, and his wife smiled at one another as they too wandered the grounds of Tŷ Mynydd.

Across the way, the master of the estate, one Mr. Nickolas Pritchard, a one-time impoverished gentleman, and his ladywife, known to her nearest and dearest simply as Gwen, watched the goings-on with smiles of amusement.

Such apparent happiness was expected amongst newlyweds who are terribly in love with one another and have found it necessary to fight off evildoers and centuries-old curses in order to be together. Their staff oohed and ahhed at their obvious affection.

The Pritchards, after countless hours spent in expressing profound gratitude at the happy outcome of the struggle nearly to the death that had brought Gwen back to life and the two of them into each other's arms, had settled between themselves that life was excessively good. Gwen was still plagued on occasion by nightmares of her harrowing experiences and had the unfortunate tendency to walk into walls when not paying attention. She was, however, so inarguably happy that all who saw her were immediately convinced of her contentment.

The Tower and a certain anguished angel in the churchyard had both been toppled within days of their life-and-death struggle. Nickolas instructed workers to set the stones of the demolished Tower in the outline of the once-fortified castle as a lasting reminder of the life Gwen had known. More touching even than that was the painting he had commissioned of Y Castell as she chose to remember it—peaceful and alive.

And there they stood, a year to the date that the ancient curse on the estate had been broken, scandalously wrapped in each other's arms.

"This has worked even better than I anticipated," Gwen said, leaning into her husband's embrace as best she could, considering the ever-expanding nature of her waistline, a *condition* she was nearly as overjoyed about as was her husband. "I am amazed so many have come. We did not write to that many people."

"Ah, but it was not the quantity of messages that made the difference, my dearest love," her husband answered, showing more open affection than was strictly proper out in the open and surrounded by hordes of humanity.

Gwen gave him a look of reproof he completely ignored, in response to which she muttered an imprecating evaluation of his manners as they related to his English heritage. She did so in Welsh and, watching the amused grin on his face, once again rued the fact that she'd taught him to be relatively proficient in her native tongue.

"Then what was the ingredient that made this day such a rousing success?" Gwen asked.

Nickolas shrugged. "The postscript."

She didn't dare ask. Gwen had learned over the eleven months she'd been Mrs. Nickolas Pritchard that such obvious traps were best left alone, though she smiled despite herself.

Nickolas, knowing his wife was too experienced with his wit to take the bait he had so temptingly dangled before her, simply answered the question she had not asked.

"I concluded my letters by telling the recipients that, though I am by all accounts still rather too English to truly understand such things, I was quite certain no *Nos Galan Gaeaf* celebration in all of Wales was quite as teeming with ghosts and mysteries and heroic opportunities as here at Tŷ Mynydd. And I may also have mentioned the child-eating sow."

Gwen gave her husband a look of amused surprise.

He shrugged as though he'd said nothing unusual. "I strongly suggested to those I wrote that they'd not want to miss a celebration so rife with specters. Unless, of course, they lacked the required courage to endure such a thing."

It was, if one was being technical, a touch misleading. The house and grounds were not rife with ghosts and would not be, despite the fact that it was *Nos Galan Gaeaf*. Tŷ Mynydd no longer housed even a single specter.

The curse was broken.

The master of the estate had inherited wealth and property and had found a loving and beloved wife. And, as Nickolas could have told any of his friends or acquaintances, of all he had gained in the past year, *she* was the true treasure.

About the Author

SARAH M. EDEN READ HER first Jane Austen novel in elementary school and has been an Austen addict ever since. Fascinated by the English Regency era, Eden became a regular in that section of the reference department at her local library, where she painstakingly researched this extraordinary chapter in history. Eden is an award-winning author of short stories and was a Whitney Award finalist for her novels *Seeking Persephone* and *Courting Miss Lancaster*. Visit her at www.sarahmeden.com.